Will
at the
Battle of
Gettysburg
1863

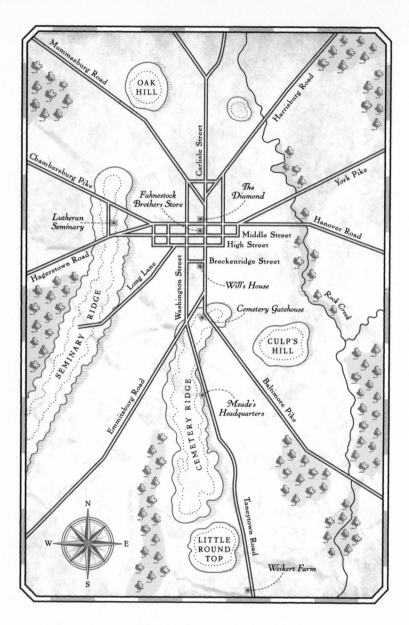

* MAP *of* GETTYSBURG 1863 *

★ BOYS OF WARTIME ★

Will
at the
Battle of
Gettysburg
1863

LAURIE CALKHOVEN

DUTTON CHILDREN'S BOOKS

An imprint of Penguin Group (USA) Inc.

For Chris DuBois and Martha Levine, two warm and generous friends, who were willing to cart a non-driver around the battlefield. Thank you, thank you, thank you!

✶

DUTTON CHILDREN'S BOOKS
A division of Penguin Young Readers Group
Published by the Penguin Group ∗ Penguin Group (USA) Inc., 375 Hudson Street, New York, New York 10014, U.S.A. ∗ Penguin Group (Canada), 90 Eglinton Avenue East, Suite 700, Toronto, Ontario M4P 2Y3, Canada (a division of Pearson Penguin Canada Inc.) ∗ Penguin Books Ltd, 80 Strand, London WC2R 0RL, England ∗ Penguin Ireland, 25 St Stephen's Green, Dublin 2, Ireland (a division of Penguin Books Ltd) ∗ Penguin Group (Australia), 250 Camberwell Road, Camberwell, Victoria 3124, Australia (a division of Pearson Australia Group Pty Ltd) ∗ Penguin Books India Pvt Ltd, 11 Community Centre, Panchsheel Park, New Delhi - 110 017, India ∗ Penguin Group (NZ), 67 Apollo Drive, Rosedale, North Shore 0632, New Zealand (a division of Pearson New Zealand Ltd.) ∗ Penguin Books (South Africa) (Pty) Ltd, 24 Sturdee Avenue, Rosebank, Johannesburg 2196, South Africa ∗ Penguin Books Ltd, Registered Offices: 80 Strand, London WC2R 0RL, England

Although this is a work of fiction, many of the historical events portrayed and persons named are real. The author has used history as a stage for several fictitious characters, and any resemblance of those characters to actual people is unintentional.

Copyright © 2011 by Laurie Calkhoven

The publisher does not have any control over and does not assume any responsibility for author or third-party websites or their content.

CIP Data is available.

Published in the United States by Dutton Children's Books,
a division of Penguin Young Readers Group
345 Hudson Street, New York, New York 10014
www.penguin.com/youngreaders

Interior and Map design by Jason Henry
Printed in the United States
First Edition ∗ ISBN 978-0-525-42145-0
1 3 5 7 9 10 8 6 4 2

Civil War *noun* 1. A war between citizens of the
same country.

—— ✯ ——

"A house divided against itself cannot stand."
—Abraham Lincoln, JUNE 1858

★ CONTENTS ★

	PROLOGUE: A TOWN AT THE CROSSROADS	3
1	A PATCH OF GROUND	7
2	A SECRET RAILROAD	15
3	SPRINGING TO THE CALL	22
4	REBEL CAVALRY!	29
5	FIGHTING FOR THE CAUSE	44
6	A REBEL AT THE SUPPER TABLE	52
7	INTOLERABLE SUSPENSE	62
8	STORYBOOK KNIGHTS	68
9	A DANCE WITH THE ENEMY	73
10	A FAMILY SEPARATED	83
11	"TO YOUR CELLAR!"	92
12	A RISKY PLAN	101
13	WHITE FLAGS	109
14	DR. EDMONDS	116
15	THE WEIKERT FARM	127
16	ANOTHER TASK	135
17	THE SNAPPING TURTLE	142
18	A REB PRISONER	151

19	"THIS'LL DECIDE IT!"	164
20	BY THE DAWN'S EARLY LIGHT	172
21	"WHERE IS MY MOTHER?"	180
22	REUNIONS	187
23	A NEW BIRTH OF FREEDOM	200
	Historical Note	208
	Children's Roles in the Civil War	211
	Historic Characters	213
	Timeline	217
	Glossary	226
	Further Reading	229
	Acknowledgments	230

Will
at the
Battle of
Gettysburg
1863

✦

A Town at
the Crossroads

W hen the Founding Fathers of the United States gathered to write the Constitution that would govern their new country, they argued most fiercely over two things. First, how much independence should each state have? And second, should slavery be abolished or allowed to spread?

Over time, those two arguments only grew worse. The South wanted to keep their slaves. Northern states made slavery illegal. Then Abraham Lincoln, an antislavery candidate, was elected President of the United States. Southern states were afraid the federal government would take their power away and force them to set their slaves free.

By the time Abraham Lincoln was inaugurated in 1861, seven Southern states had announced they were seceding, leaving the United States to form their own country. They called themselves the Confederate States of America. They were later joined by four more Southern states.

The North, led by Abraham Lincoln, declared secession illegal and a danger to the whole country. It would not be allowed. A war between the Union of the North and the Confederacy of the South began.

The American Civil War was in its third year by the summer of 1863, and things didn't look good for the Union. Even though Robert E. Lee's Confederate army was outnumbered by Union troops and short of food and weapons, they defeated the Union army over and over again.

On the heels of a victory in Chancellorsville, Virginia, Lee decided to march his army north. His plan was to cut Washington—the North's capital city—off from the rest of the country. He hoped that a Union defeat in its own territory would force President Lincoln to bring the war to an end and allow the Confederate states to secede from the Union. Along the way, the undamaged farms of Maryland and Pennsylvania would feed Lee's hungry army.

Just over the Maryland border, the small town of

Gettysburg, Pennsylvania, sat at the center of ten major roads. No one intended to fight there. In fact, the commanders of both armies had never even heard of the town of twenty-four-hundred people. But the citizens of Gettysburg were about to find themselves caught between two armies in the biggest, bloodiest battle of the war.

★ CHAPTER ONE ★

A Patch of Ground

Tuesday, June 16, 1863

The battlefield had no name that I knew of. Just a patch of ground somewhere in Virginia where our men fell up against some Rebs. Someone fired and soon there was an all-out battle. Messengers galloped to us, urging our company to hurry. The general at my side ordered me to signal the men to march on the double-quick.

I rattled my drum as we ran forward. The drumbeats urged the men to move faster. I could hear shells bursting ahead of us, along with muskets firing and the groans of men who got hit.

Suddenly, we were upon it.

My general nodded to me and I drummed the order to charge.

Rat-a-tat-tat. Rat-a-tat-tat.

Our color-bearer waved the Stars and Stripes, leading the men into battle. I was proud to see that there wasn't a coward among us.

All was chaos. Smoke from the heavy artillery guns made it impossible to see. A shell landed near my feet, and I dove behind a tree before it could explode and take my life. The smoke cleared just for a moment. A line of gray and steel advanced toward us like a serpent in the grass.

Then I saw it. Our flag was falling. Our color-bearer had been hit. I threw off my drum and dashed to him, dodging bullets that flew thicker than bees. I caught the flag just before it hit the ground. I would sooner die than have the Stars and Stripes fall into the hands of those who wanted to destroy the Union.

The color-bearer gazed at me with grateful eyes, and then slumped over dead.

I raised the flag high. "Courage, men!" I shouted.

The men had faltered. Now they rallied.

The general ran beside me, waving his sword. "There'll be a medal in this for you, boy, if—"

"William Joseph Edmonds," my mother

screeched. "If you don't stop your woolgathering and help me, I will tan your hide."

Her words jerked me right out of my daydream. I wasn't on a battlefield. I was sitting at our kitchen table.

The twins, Sally and Jane Ann, set to giggling. They were just five, an age when the idea of a hide tanning was pure entertainment—if the hide was not one of their own.

My fifteen-year-old sister, Grace, tugged me to my feet by the tuft of hair that was forever standing up on the top of my head. Bossy, she was. She dropped a smoked ham into my arms. "Will, take this to the cellar and hide it in the ash barrel."

Mother had more chores. "And then ride Molasses to the Bailey farm. See if they can hide her along with their own horses. The Rebels will steal every horse they can."

Mother was packing the good silver with the help of the twins. Her jewelry was already wrapped in a rag and hidden in a nook in the garret.

I got to work, although I didn't see the purpose. At least every other week since the war began someone rode through town with the news that the Rebels were coming.

They never did.

Nearest they got was Latshaw's Tavern when Jeb Stuart came into Pennsylvania with a raiding party last fall. They were back on the Southern side of Mason and Dixon's line before we even knew they were there.

Not that I would mind fighting the Rebs. There were plenty of twelve-year-old drummers. I saw no reason why I couldn't be one of them. I would have gladly mustered in with my brother, Jacob, when he went to be a soldier. But the government said you had to be eighteen to sign up without a parent's permission, and there was no way mine would allow it.

I had to content myself with reading the newspaper accounts of battles in places like Bull Run and Antietam, and, just recently, Chancellorsville. Sometimes the men in town had long, dull talks about the causes of the war, and some folks said the fighting wasn't even worth it. I still didn't understand why the South thought they could just bust up the country.

I followed Jacob's movements on the map on our parlor table, wishing I could be there with him to help save the Union.

His letters were mostly about the food and the drills; he left out all the exciting parts. Maybe he was trying to spare Mother and Grace from worrying, but those letters sure were boring. As far as I could tell, he had done nothing heroic. Then he got captured in Fredericksburg, Virginia. We got a letter from a Southern lady who had nursed him, informing us that he had been transferred from an army hospital to a prison camp, and then no more. Father took the train to Washington two months ago to see if he could get Jacob released in a prisoner exchange, but he's had no luck as of yet. While he waits, Father signed on to be a doctor in one of the army hospitals there.

I tried to be the man in the family and make him proud, but Grace seemed to think that was her job. The only thing I got to do was pack away hams and hide our horse in case the Rebs marched into town.

This time the governor had issued a proclamation urging the people to organize and defend the state. A few days later, he telegraphed a warning directing us to move our valuables out of town.

Fahnestock Brothers and other stores filled railroad cars with goods to ship to Philadelphia. The cashier at the bank packed the cash and valuables in a valise and was ready to run. So were the postmaster and the telegraph operator. The roads were clogged with farmers, their horses, and other livestock. Wagons were filled with whatever crops that had come in. Everyone knew the Rebel army was hungry. They would eat every last thing they got their hands on if they invaded.

I felt sorriest for the Negroes. It seemed like every other week they had to sling everything they owned on their backs and hightail it up Baltimore Street for the woods beyond Culp's Hill. The Rebels were known to capture them and sell them in the slave markets down south—even those who had been born on free soil and had always been free.

Aunt Bess, the woman who helped Mother with her cleaning and her washing, was ailing. Mother tried to convince her to stay with the promise that she would hide Bess if the Rebels came anywhere near.

"I ain't going to risk it," Aunt Bess had said. "I'd rather die an early death as a free woman than live a hundred more years as a slave in the South."

I wouldn't argue with that. I believed that slavery was evil through and through, but I still thought the town was in an uproar over nothing.

Even so, I hid my own treasures. I opened my box and looked everything over: half a package of

Necco Wafers I had hidden from the twins, a genuine Indian arrowhead, my spelling medal, drumsticks (Mother wouldn't let me have a drum), the ten cents I was saving for the next time Owen Robinson cranked out ice cream at his confectionery, and my slingshot. On second thought, I slipped my slingshot into my pocket. Maybe I'd use it to scare some Rebs, if they ever did take it into their heads to show up.

For days, folks did little more than stand around the street, sharing rumors. Last night the sky glowed red with flames. Emmitsburg, Maryland, was on fire. Folks were screaming, "The Rebels are coming, and they're burning as they go!"

This morning our neighbor Mr. Pierce came by with the news. "It wasn't the Rebs," he told us. "Some crazy firebug set his own town ablaze. Can you imagine that?"

I couldn't and I was glad we didn't have anyone like that living in our town. "So the Rebs aren't coming?" I asked.

"Robert E. Lee's cavalry crossed the Potomac and are in Chambersburg," Mr. Pierce said. His expression was grim.

Grace gasped. "Chambersburg! That's just twenty-five miles from here."

Mr. Pierce turned to me. "I think it's best you get that horse of yours to a safe hiding place. Your father will need him when he gets back from Washington."

I already had orders to do that right after lunch, but the last thing I needed was for Grace to get herself into even more of a flap over this latest piece of news.

"Aww, I don't believe they're coming here," I said. "What would the Rebels want with a place like Gettysburg, Pennsylvania?"

CHAPTER TWO

A Secret Railroad

I was pleased to get away from the womenfolk for a while. Grace was a student at Mrs. Eyster's Young Ladies Seminary, and as far as I could tell all they taught her was how to be a major irritation. You'd think the world would come to an end if a fellow put his elbows on the table or forgot to use his napkin to wipe his mouth.

Grace had become more and more high-handed since Jacob left. He was five years older than her, and could tease her into giving a fellow a break. I sure missed him. Jacob taught me things and treated me like a man. Grace just ordered me around.

Now that Father, too, was gone she was close to intolerable. You'd think she was in charge of the family.

Today she yelled instructions while I saddled Molasses for the ride to the Bailey farm. Mother had packed me a cold dinner, as it would be a long walk back. With any luck, I'd get something delicious to eat from Mrs. Bailey, too. Her pies were prizewinners.

"You headed out to hide that horse, Will?" Mrs. Shriver asked me as I rode by.

I owned that I was.

"Be careful out there. The Rebs could be anywhere."

"Yes, ma'am," I said. A fellow couldn't get a break from women and their orders wherever he went.

I rode down Baltimore Street and around the town square—we called it the Diamond—on my way to the Carlisle Road. Small clumps of townspeople shared the latest rumors. Some gathered at the newspaper offices. I knew others would be standing around the telegraph at the railroad station. I had done a lot of that when the war first started, waiting for news of Jacob.

As soon as we were out of town, I let Molasses have her lead. She was a good horse, accustomed to going fast when Father had an emergency call to the country. She knew her way to the Bailey place practically better than I did. Before the war started, old Mrs. Bailey used to get sick a lot. Father rode out to their farm two or three times a month.

About eight months before the war began, he headed out there just after supper one night. I went along, sitting beside him in the buggy in the hopes of having a practice game of baseball with Calvin Bailey, old Mrs. Bailey's grandson, before it got too dark. Baseball was the new craze among boys in town, and I wasn't very good yet.

When we got there, Cal was nowhere to be seen. Father bid me to wait in the buggy until someone came to fetch me. I wondered why he was acting so mysterious, but I did as I was told.

I sat for a long time. It was a warm summer night. The stars came out along with a full moon. I heard a barn owl hoot and turned to try to find it. That's when I saw Cal.

"Cal!" I yelled. "Think it's too dark for a game before I go?"

He stopped short, scared like, and that's when I

saw there were people behind him. Negroes. Four of them. A man had a white bandage around his arm, bright in the moonlight. A woman put her hand over her mouth. Two children each clutched something. It looked like they were holding the kind of rag dolls Grace was forever making. Father said he carried them to give to sick children. I never imagined he was giving them to runaway slave children.

It pained me to see them act so scared at the sight of me. "Never . . . never mind," I said to Cal. "I see you've got chores."

Cal nodded. The Negro man's shoulders slumped in relief and the group continued on their way, slipping into the barn. I knew slaves used secret escape routes to make their way north to freedom. Folks called it the Underground Railroad. There were rumors of such in Gettysburg, but this was the first time I knew about it for sure. I was proud of Father for doing his part.

I never spoke of it. Not to Father. Not to Cal. Not to anyone. But I checked Father's medical kit when we got home, and the dolls I knew to be there earlier in the day were gone. The Bailey family suddenly got healthier when the war began. Father stopped making as many trips out to the farm. I guess the war made it too dangerous for most slaves to escape.

Today was another hot summer day, and this time I made the trip without Father. There would be no baseball, either. The Bailey family had even more to protect from the Rebels than we did, so Cal was kept hard at work. The family had to get whatever crops in they could before the Rebs showed up, and hide all their livestock every time some fool said the Rebs were coming.

It was like all the fun had gone out of summer and been replaced by worry. Seemed to me that as long as there was a war on, I should be in it, doing something useful.

I spurred Molasses along. If I didn't get to the farm before Mr. Bailey and Cal left with their own horses, Grace wouldn't stop screeching for a week.

Mrs. Bailey stepped onto her front porch when she heard me coming.

"Are you taking your horses away, Mrs. Bailey?" I asked. "Mother wanted to see if you could take our Molasses, too."

"You're welcome to leave her with us, Will," she said. "Our animals are still here, but Mr. Bailey and Cal will ride out with them before too long.

We'll keep her out of their hands if we can."

"Thank you," I said. "When Father was at home we always kept her with us. We expected even the Rebs would let a doctor keep his horse. But with him in Washington, they'll grab her sure."

"Any news from your father?" she asked.

I shook my head, then looked around for Cal, or one of the farmhands. "Where is everyone?"

"Out haying. They headed out again right after the noon meal," she said. "Getting in as much of the crop as we can before the Rebels come. If they come."

"I don't believe they will," I said. "Robert E. Lee likes to let us think he's coming just to cause a commotion. He's probably somewhere down in Virginia having a good laugh."

"Maybe so," she said. "You get that horse to the barn and then stop by the kitchen for some cherry pie and a cold drink before you leave."

Just what I was hoping for! "Yes, ma'am," I told her.

I promised Molasses I'd come back for her as soon as the Rebel threat was proved false. After having my fill of cherry pie, I walked the five miles back to Gettysburg. All along, I imagined what I would do if the Rebels suddenly appeared.

I'd spot them from a distance, and then I'd climb the tallest tree I could find. I'd take aim at the lead soldiers with my slingshot. One, two, three, I'd hit them with rocks right in the middle of their foreheads.

"Turn around, boys!" the officer in command would shout. "I don't know where these bullets are coming from, but we must be outnumbered."

All three newspapers in town would call me a hero. My name would be splashed across the front page.

With that in mind I filled my pockets with rocks and then climbed a tree to scan the countryside. I saw nothing but farmers working in their fields.

I got home to find the same groups of people on the same corners talking about the same Rebel invasion. The words "bloody and desperate foe" were printed in big letters on the front page of the Democrat newspaper. Both Republican papers carried the same kind of warnings.

The only battle I had was with Grace. She yelled at me for dawdling on my way home and worrying Mother.

★ CHAPTER THREE ★

Springing to the Call

Tuesday, June 16, 1863

T illie Pierce, who heard it from Mrs. Pierce, who heard it from Mrs. Shriver, told Grace that Gettysburg's young men were down at Buehler's Drug and Bookstore taking the oath to be emergency infantry volunteers. As soon as her back was turned, I snuck up to the garret to get my drumsticks.

I ran down Baltimore Street thinking of how Mother would surely say yes since this was an emergency, especially if I was already signed up.

The flag on the pole in the middle of the Diamond flapped in the breeze. It made my heart swell with pride at the thought of defending the Stars and Stripes. Surely the emergency troops would need a drummer.

Buehler's was on the first block of Chambersburg Street, just off the Diamond. A crowd of college boys and a few Lutheran Seminary men milled around out front, along with some town boys. This was usually where the two sets came to fight, often over some girl. Today they were slapping each other on their backs, acting all jovial. A few strutted around like roosters, trying to catch the eyes of the girls across the street.

The girls stood there in a gaggle. One or two dabbed their eyes with handkerchiefs. A couple of them were friends of Grace's, so I ducked my head quick and turned my back to them. I didn't want Grace ruining my plans before Mother had a chance to say yes.

There was a man from Harrisburg in the middle of the volunteers, taking down names. "You all need a drummer?" I asked.

One or two of them smiled at me like I was daft.

I pulled my sticks out of my back pocket. "I have

my own copy of *The Drummers' and Fifers' Guide*, and I've been practicing."

The name-taker eyed me up and down. "How old are you?"

"Almost thirteen," I said, standing as tall as I could. "The name's Will Edmonds."

"You have your parents' permission to muster in?" he asked.

I nodded. I figured if I didn't say the words out loud it wasn't quite a lie. Besides, I'd have permission soon.

I was getting ready to sign the papers when a hand broke through the crowd and tugged me by the hair.

Grace screeched at me. "William Edmonds! What do you think you're doing?"

My cheeks burned. There were chuckles all around. I heard an "uh-oh."

Grace's eyes flashed.

The college boys puffed out their chests a little more.

Grace paid them no mind. She dragged me across the street to the womenfolk, squawking the whole time. "You know Mother can't stand any more worry right now."

I glared at her and kicked the sidewalk. "I was

only going to muster in for the emergency," I told her. "Not for the whole dang war."

"Go on home," Grace said. "Right now."

Charlie McCurdy was in front of his house watching my mortification. I kicked the sidewalk again and crossed the street to avoid him. I thought a piece of candy might soothe my hurt pride, but I didn't even have a penny in my pocket to spend at Petey Winter's candy store.

I heard a cheer behind me. I guess all those would-be preachers had taken the oath. The girls started singing "The Battle Cry of Freedom."

> *Yes, we'll rally round the flag, boys,*
> *we'll rally once again,*
> > *Shouting the battle cry of freedom,*
> > *We will rally from the hillside,*
> *we'll gather from the plain,*
> > *Shouting the battle cry of Freedom.*
> > *The Union forever! Hurrah, boys, hurrah!*
> > *Down with the traitors, up with the stars;*
> > *While we rally round the flag, boys,*
> *rally once again,*
> > *Shouting the battle cry of freedom!*

The boys joined in for the last verse:

*So we're springing to the call from the East
and from the West,*
    Shouting the battle cry of freedom!
    *And we'll hurl the rebel crew from the land
that we love best,*
    Shouting the battle cry of freedom!

I blocked my ears to keep from hearing any more. The breeze had died and the Stars and Stripes in the Diamond hung limp and sad.

If Father were here he'd want me to join up. So would Jacob. There was no way I'd be snatched up by any Rebels and get taken to prison. I'd fight to the death. I would make Gettysburg and Pennsylvania proud—if only someone would let me.

Two days later the new soldiers marched off to Harrisburg for training, singing still. Most of them had had their pictures made at Tyson's gallery to leave with their mothers or their sweethearts. They were named Company A of the Twenty-sixth Pennsylvania Emergency Volunteer Infantry. A greener bunch of troops I never saw.

Major Haller from the War Department rode into town to tell us to arm ourselves. A local farmer, Robert Bell, made himself a captain and raised a company of independent cavalry. I wondered about going back to the Baileys' to fetch Molasses, but Grace struck that idea down before I even finished thinking it.

"You'll not be joining them, Will," she told me. "That horse is staying wherever the Baileys have hidden her."

Mother and Grace wouldn't even let me go with the town men who marched out to the Chambersburg Pike with axes on their shoulders. They aimed to chop down some trees and block the mountain passes to slow the Rebel advance. They came back pretty quick though. The Rebels surprised us all. They had already marched through the Cashtown Gap and were on our side of the mountain.

Rebels! The news shot through my body like lightning. Maybe I'd get to do some fighting after all. That night, I saw their campfires on the slopes of South Mountain. I wondered how many of them were out there, and whether or not the Union army was coming to wage a battle.

Not much happened in the next few days. We were in a state of high alert, but the Rebels stayed put. Bell's scouts rode back and forth, keeping an eye on the Rebs but never getting within shooting range. A telegram came from Harrisburg to tell us that the Twenty-sixth Emergency Volunteers were coming back by train to defend the town. I still didn't believe the Rebels would favor us with a visit. There were a lot of other places they could go. The state capital at Harrisburg seemed more likely.

In between chores I ran back and forth from the telegraph office to the newspaper offices to get scraps of news. No one knew what to expect.

Charlie McCurdy had made a little cannon out of a piece of gas pipe. It was about a foot long and mounted on a block of wood. We fired pebbles until Mrs. McCurdy said, "For heavens sake, don't we have enough to worry about," and took it away. That was the most fun I had all week long.

If the Rebels were truly coming, I wished they would get here already.

★ CHAPTER FOUR ★

Rebel Cavalry!

Friday, June 26, 1863

The Twenty-sixth didn't get back to Gettys-burg until Friday morning on account of their train hitting a cow and getting derailed. I couldn't see how four days of army training would ready them for Robert E. Lee, but they marched in pleased as punch with themselves, mooning for the girls. I wouldn't act so ridiculous if I were one of them. Even with all their preening, folks bent over backward to sing them songs and feed them breakfast.

Before noon they marched out again behind

Captain Bell's cavalry. I itched to follow them, but Grace and Mother were both watching me pretty close.

I stood around with everyone else, waiting to see what would happen. Mr. Pierce said he hoped that the Rebels had raided the countryside for their fill of Pennsylvania crops and had already turned back around.

But that's not what happened.

The next thing we knew, Bell's cavalry was galloping down Chambersburg Street like chickens with a fox behind them.

"Rebel cavalry is on our heels!" someone yelled as they raced by.

I ran behind them as fast as I could. They pulled up at the Diamond. "Our boys were no match for them," one of the riders said. "The Twenty-sixth is in full retreat. The Rebels are riding on Gettysburg with at least a brigade of infantry behind them."

Someone gasped. "A brigade, that's five thousand soldiers."

I couldn't believe it. A whole brigade of Rebs riding on Gettysburg.

Bell and his men spurred their horses and galloped out of town, leaving us without any military protection at all. I was struck dumb with the shock of it.

I ran to the foot of Chambersburg Street and trained my eyes on Seminary Ridge, a half mile away. It wasn't long before I saw a horseman crest the ridge. Behind him a dark mass moved toward town, like a river about to overflow its banks. Would they swallow us up?

Some girls ran past me helter-skelter, and I noted that the front portico of Mrs. Eyster's Young Ladies Seminary was full of even more girls. I found Grace and we ran the two blocks home together with Tillie Pierce.

Mother pulled Grace and me into the house and slammed the door. We peeked out from between the shutters in the parlor. I tried to think of where I could find a weapon. Father wasn't a hunter, nor was Jacob. We didn't have a gun in the house. I wished we had a musket—two muskets. Grace could load one while I fired the other through the window. *Pow! Pow! Pow!* The Rebs wouldn't know what hit them.

Suddenly the Rebs thundered down Baltimore Street! They screamed and hollered and shot their guns into the air like savages from beyond the Rocky Mountains. I had read newspaper accounts of the Rebel yell, but it didn't prepare me for the unearthly, high-pitched sound they made. It traveled up my spine like a ghost's howl, setting my hair on end.

I thought, *They'd as soon cut your throat as give you the time of day.* I wished Father were here, and Jacob. They would know what to do.

I could only stare out the window as the enemy rode by, whooping and hollering. Finally they slowed down some; then I could see how sorry looking they were. They sat high and proud in their saddles, but they were covered in dust and wearing only rags. One rider had spurs attached to bare ankles!

Some local boys and their horses were being led like prisoners at the back of the line. They must have gotten caught trying to hurry the animals out of town when the Rebs came upon them. One of the boys was Sam Wade, the Pierces' hired help. I could hear Mrs. Pierce call out.

"You don't want the boy! You have our horse. Let the boy go," she said.

The Rebel answered as polite as could be. "No, we don't want the boy, you can have him. We're only after horses."

With that the Reb let go of Sam, who ran like the dickens for Mrs. Pierce.

I poked my head out the window, ready to yank it back in at the first sign of a gun pointed in my direction. Grace tried to pull me back in, but I shook her off. I saw a huge dust cloud moving toward town. That must be the infantry Bell's rider spoke of. Five thousand soldiers. I was scared and excited all at the same time.

Mrs. Pierce and Mrs. Shriver were on the sidewalk in front of the Pierce house. Sam stood between them looking like he might collapse at any moment. I guess the Rebs scared him pretty bad.

The enemy cavalry had wheeled around the Diamond and then charged out again, raising dust and whooping and hollering. They paid no notice to me, or to the townspeople who ventured out onto the street. They were mostly interested in putting on a show. It didn't seem like there was any danger at all.

Grace took Sally and Jane Ann out to the privy. I saw my chance to ask Mother for leave to go to the Diamond without Grace's interference. Old Mrs. Duncan lived alone just past the Christ Lutheran Church on Chambersburg Street. She was a favorite of Mother's, and I pointed out how she might be scared. I offered to go and get her and bring her to our house.

"That's very thoughtful of you, Will. But Mrs. Duncan won't want you to put yourself in danger."

"No danger," I said. "They let Sam go. They're not hurting any of the folks on the street. And Mrs. Duncan must be mighty scared."

Mother sighed in that sad way she had since Jacob got snatched by the Rebs. "Be extra careful," she said. "Don't do anything foolish."

I assured her I wouldn't and stepped into the street before Grace could ruin everything. The dust cloud was even bigger now. Five thousand marching men sure did stir up a lot of dirt.

When I got down to the Diamond I learned that the Rebels had demanded money, food, and other supplies. The town council was meeting at Mr. William Duncan's office. A Rebel general sat on his horse on the first block of Baltimore Street waiting for their reply.

"He'll burn the whole town down if they don't get what they want," someone whispered. "That's what they did in Carlisle."

I decided to wait and see what would happen before I looked for Mrs. Duncan.

By then the first of the infantry soldiers had reached the center of town. It was hard to believe that any outfit could be in worse shape than the cavalry, but these foot soldiers were even more ragged.

I saw a drummer about my age without any shoes at all. He was slumped against David Wills's house, his tongue hanging out as if he needed water. His trousers had so many holes in them that you couldn't even rightly call them trousers. And I didn't see a trace of underwear. Grace would turn the deepest shade of red if she got a look at him from behind.

I'm not a big supporter of baths, but this fellow looked like he hadn't had one since the war began. I almost felt sorry for him. Then I remembered he was my enemy.

Mr. Kendlehart, our council president, came out and told the Rebel general that Gettysburg couldn't meet his demands. Everything had been shipped out of town. He invited the soldiers to inspect the town's stores to see what they could find. I guess that satisfied them. No one set fire to anything, and soon the Rebs were going from store to store, emptying the shelves. They took everything they could carry. One soldier had a pile of hats on his head. Another trailed blankets and shawls from his shoulders.

They paid for everything with their Confederate money.

One of the storekeepers objected. "I want good money," he said.

"In two months time our money will be better than your greenbacks," a soldier answered with a sneer. "We'll be remaining in your state for some time."

I gave him my dirtiest look. The war hadn't been going so well for the Union army, but I didn't believe they'd allow the Rebs to stay up north. They'd drive them back down south for sure.

The Rebels were sure enjoying our town now. They prowled the streets like hungry wolves. A couple of them forced Petey Winters to open the shutters on his sweet shop. In seconds the Rebs cleared out all the molasses taffy and ginger cakes he had. I watched through the store window with Charlie McCurdy. One Reb came out with a hat full of penny candy and dropped some into Charlie's hand and then into mine. I almost threw it back at him, but I didn't know when I'd see sweets again if the Rebels stuck around like they said they would. I sucked on one and slipped the rest into my pocket.

When I finally got to Mrs. Duncan's, I discovered that she had taken one of the last trains to her daughter's home in New Jersey.

When I turned back to the Diamond to head on home, I saw that the Rebels had pulled down our flag. An officer stood on the Union flag in his Rebel boots and raised the Confederate flag over our town while they sang a Rebel song:

> *Then I wish I was in Dixie! Hooray! Hooray!*
> *In Dixie Land I'll take my stand, to live and*
> *die in Dixie!*
> *Away! Away! Away down South in Dixie!*
> *Away! Away! Away down South in Dixie!*

Anger rushed through me like fire in a hayloft. I wanted to charge right over, knock that Rebel down, and save the Stars and Stripes. I imagined the whole town rallying behind me. We'd force those Rebels to stop singing their Confederate airs and take down their flag.

But I didn't. When you got down to it, there were five thousand Rebel soldiers and only a couple of thousand Gettysburg folks. We were no match for them.

The Rebels were so packed together on Baltimore Street that I couldn't even see a space between them. Dirt and sweat rose off their bodies and created a horrible stink. Instead I headed down Chambersburg toward Washington Street where it was less crowded.

I heard someone shouting up ahead and made my way through a small group of laughing Rebs. Truth to tell, a couple of Gettysburg folks were laughing, too. I gasped when I saw what they were laughing at.

Three ugly soldiers had lined up about a dozen Negroes.

"Dance old man," one of the Rebels ordered. "If you don't have the energy to give a master a good day's work, we might have to shoot you here instead of marching you all the way back to Virginia."

Old Mr. Carter, tears pouring down his face, slowly began to dance.

"How much you think he'll fetch, Joe?" the Rebel asked.

The one called Joe shrugged and scratched his

neck. "A hundred, maybe two. Better than nothing."

I searched the faces around me, waiting for one of the grown-ups to do something. Their eyes met mine and then slid away. They stared at their feet and stood silent.

Aunt Bess was among the Negroes. Why hadn't she left town? She held her head high and dignified. Others were crying and moaning. Mr. Nutter held tight to his grandson Basil's hand. I knew for a fact that Mr. Nutter had his freedom papers from his old master in Maryland, and Basil had been born right here on free soil. These were free people.

Joe put his hand on Basil's shoulder and eyed him up and down like he was livestock at a farm sale. "Found this one hiding in a chicken coop," he laughed. "We'll have to wash off that chicken poop before we bring him to auction." He looked Basil in the eyes. "What do you think, chicken? We've got a shortage of young bucks. I bet you'll sell for a thousand dollars or more."

Basil's eyes were on fire. He clenched his jaw and said nothing.

The woman next to him dropped to her knees and begged to be killed right then and there.

Joe laughed and pointed his musket at her. "I'd be happy to oblige," he drawled, "but I need the cash you'll fetch."

My heart twisted in my chest. Where was the town council? Why didn't anyone do anything to stop this? I watched Aunt Bess. There was a sadness so deep in her eyes that I couldn't bear it. Before I knew it I was running toward Joe, screaming my head off in my own kind of Rebel yell. I kept my head down, but I saw feet scattering. I could only hope some of them belonged to the Negroes.

The next thing I knew I was flat on my back with a Rebel boot on my chest. There was a hole in the shoe, and I could see Joe's crusty, dirty toes. I tried to lift my head, but he held it down with the business end of his musket.

"Look what I've got here," he drawled. "One of those Yankee abolitionists. You know what we do with abolitionists, don't you, boy?" he asked.

I couldn't answer. I waited for the shot that would end my life. All the noise around me stopped. My eyes were locked on his face—on the hatred in it. The Courthouse clock struck the four o'clock hour.

I closed my eyes. Every muscle in my body froze up. I couldn't even swallow.

"Be extra careful," Mother had said. It pained me to think that her last memory of me would be one of me disobeying. Tears began to leak out of my eyes.

"I'll take him, Cap'n," a voice said. It was liquid, Southern, and high like a boy's.

The boot pressure lifted a bit, but Joe was still ready to stomp the life out of me, or shoot me, or both. His musket still held my head to the ground.

"I'll take him to the Courthouse over yonder," the voice said. It was nearer now. "With the other prisoners. They'll make sure he doesn't cause any more trouble."

The speaker came into my range of vision. It was the drummer I had seen earlier, the one with more holes than trousers.

"Who are you?" Captain Joe demanded.

I was relieved to have Joe's anger directed at someone else, even for a second. My muscles thawed enough to start trembling.

"Abel Hoke, Tenth Tennessee," he replied with a nod. He waved in the direction of the Negroes.

"You keep 'em rounded up here. I'll take the boy to the Courthouse."

Joe's eyes flicked from the drummer to me and back to the drummer. His men waited to see what he would do.

Abel Hoke took another step forward and talked so quietly that only Joe and I could hear him. "We're under orders not to hurt the civilians," he said calmly. "I'll take him to the Courthouse. They'll keep him there with the prisoners."

Joe took his boot off my chest and gave me a kick in the ribs. "You cost me three slaves, boy," he spat.

I sat up, wiping the tears off my cheeks with shaking hands. The drummer stuck his hand out to pull me up, but I ignored him. I half expected Joe to change his mind and shoot me.

I guess the drummer did, too. He stepped between Joe and me and grabbed my arm.

"C'mon now," he said sternly, pulling me to my feet.

I glared at him. I hated to be crying in front of the enemy. I hated it even more that a Rebel had saved my life.

We took a few steps, and I did my best to calm

myself. I took big, shaky breaths until the urge to weep went away.

As soon as we were out of Joe's sight, I yanked my arm out of the drummer's grip. He paid me no mind, simply stuck out his hand, like he was introducing himself in church or some such thing.

"Abel Hoke from Tennessee," he said. "Pleased to make your acquaintance."

★ CHAPTER FIVE ★

Fighting for the Cause

*P*leased *to make your acquaintance?* Was this Rebel drummer trying to make friends? I stared at his hand until he dropped it.

"Don't you worry none. I'm not taking you to the Courthouse," he said, nodding. "That captain looked like a mean one. It was the only thing I could think of to get you away."

He was helping me? "Are you a Rebel?" I asked.

"A loyal Southerner." He nodded again. "Fighting for the cause."

I soon learned that he ended almost every sentence with a sharp nod, as if he was verifying the truth of his statements.

"Fighting for slavery, you mean," I corrected.

"My people don't own slaves," he said. "I'd set every last one of them free if I could."

I scratched my head, even more mystified. "Then what are you fighting for?"

"For the South," he said simply. "The North can't come into our land and tell us what's what," he said. "The South gets to decide things its own self. We don't need to be told what to do by no Yankees."

"Slavery's evil," I countered.

"You think our slaves have it worse off than the people working in your big city factories?" he asked.

I had no answer for that. I didn't know anything about factories. Or big cities. I had never even been to Philadelphia. "What about the Union?" I asked, getting kind of steamed. "All the states said they would stick together after we whipped the British in the Revolution. Seems to me that a bunch of states can't just take it into their heads to bust up the Union. It's not right.

What kind of country would we have if every time some state got mad at the others they split off from the Union?"

"Ain't much of a Union if it takes away states' rights." He was just as stubborn over the matter as I was.

"Ain't much of a state if it takes away a person's rights," I yelled.

Abel frowned. "I'm not here to fight with you," he said. "I go where the army sends me. I've got no quarrel with you."

"What if I have a quarrel with you?" I asked.

We stared at each other, contemplating a fist-fight. I was bigger than him, but he was more muscled. Plus, we were surrounded by Rebel soldiers. I was outnumbered.

I took a step toward home, ending our contest. Even so, I didn't want him to think I was scared, or beholden to him. "You didn't save my life, you know. He wasn't going to shoot me," I said. I don't know if that was true, but it felt good to say it.

"Maybe not." Abel Hoke shuffled his toes in the dirt and looked away. Something came over his face. Sadness maybe, or maybe he was just tired.

I had hurt his feelings. "I'm Will Edmonds," I said. "How long have you been a drummer?"

"Since we got news that Tennessee joined the Confederacy," he said. "I mustered in the next day. I've been a drummer ever since."

"How old were you?" He didn't look to be any older than I am, and the war started more than two years ago.

"Ten," he answered. "Almost eleven."

"And your folks let you?"

"Joined up with my daddy," he said with a nod.

"My mother and father won't let me join up," I admitted. "But I'm ready. I've been practicing my drumming."

"Your daddy a soldier?" he asked.

I had to confess that he wasn't, sure that Abel's father was a general or some such thing. "My brother, Jacob, is—was—a soldier. He's in a Southern prison. My father's down in Washington, working at an army hospital. He says the North needs doctors more than they need soldiers."

Abel nodded solemnly.

"Where's your father now?" I asked.

"Dead. Shiloh," he said matter-of-factly.

Now I looked away. Some Gettysburg boys had joined up and died in the war, but no fathers that I knew of. It crossed my mind that one day I might have to say such a thing about Jacob—

"Dead. Rebel prison."—or even Father. I couldn't imagine being able to say the words so simply. I didn't know how to answer such a statement as that.

Luckily we had reached the end of the alley. "Courthouse is this way," I said, turning onto Baltimore. "So's my house."

He stayed at my side.

Confederate soldiers were all over the street. They had stacked their muskets and built cook fires. Some girls were singing for them. It made me sick for a minute to think that they were entertaining the enemy, and then I realized they were singing a pro-Union song. The Rebs didn't seem to mind. They countered with a song of their own.

"There's the Courthouse," I said, pointing as we crossed West Middle Street.

Confederate soldiers were going in and out. Abel had said the Rebs were using it for a prison.

"We've got no call to go in there," Abel said.

"Where's your unit?" I asked. "Won't they be looking for you?"

He shrugged. "Not before dark."

I expected him to take his leave of me, but he stayed at my side. I didn't know how to ditch him.

For all my high talk, I think he may have saved my life. Then I imagined what Grace's face would look like when I showed up at home with a filthy, smelly Reb drummer boy. I smiled for the first time since the Rebels rode into town.

Abel took my smile as an invitation to ask more questions. "Do you live with your ma?"

I nodded. "My mother and three sisters, one of whom thinks she's the Queen of Sheba."

Abel sighed. "I have two sisters myself, and a little brother. I ain't seen them but once since the war started up."

I didn't know what to say to that. He got that queer faraway look again.

"My school is up this way, too," I told him. "It's vacation time, though."

"We was studying mathematics when the war broke out," he said. "And I was working on my spelling. Never could spell worth a darn."

Should I tell him about my spelling medal? I eyed him for a moment, happy to have something to make me feel superior. But he was so friendly that I didn't. "Spelling's a nuisance," I said. "Too many rules."

"One of the fellows in our unit was a teacher before the war. He helped me some. He gave me this." Abel pulled a small book out of his haver-sack. *Shakespeare's Sonnets.*

I didn't ask why the fellow didn't help him any more. I suspected he was dead, too, like Abel's father.

"I aim to go back and finish my schooling," he said firmly. "When the war's won."

I was tempted to ask, won by whom, but I didn't. I noticed Mrs. Buehler sitting on her front stoop chatting with a couple of the Rebels. Some folks were even feeding the soldiers. Everyone appeared to be downright chummy. But they were the enemy. It made my blood burn, but at the same time I was enjoying talking to Abel. Things were getting awfully confusing.

I guess Abel could see that. "We're not going to fight the people here," he said. "We're here to fight the Bluebellies. We've got no quarrel with you."

But I was for the Union. Jacob was in a Reb prison because he was for the Union. Father was in Washington for the same reason. And Abel's father was dead because he thought the South was right. So we did have a quarrel, didn't we? The whole business puzzled me to no end.

I thought about it as we walked up Baltimore Street. Albertus McCreary saw us together as we crossed High Street, and his eyes nearly fell out of his head. He watched me point out the Presbyterian Church as if I was giving a tour of the town. We passed the Pierce house and I showed Abel the tenpin alley in the back of the Shriver house. Ours was just beyond.

"That's my house," I said.

Abel's smile disappeared. He looked at the house and then away, shuffling his feet in the dirt again. His shoulders slumped over his drum, and I could see his shoulder blades sticking out like skinny twigs.

Abel was my enemy. So the next words that came out of my mouth puzzled me more than anything. "Want to stay for supper?"

★ CHAPTER SIX ★

A Rebel at the Supper Table

Want to stay for supper?
The words were hanging in the air, and I half hoped Abel would say no. That he had to get back to his unit.

"Much obliged," he said. There was a hint of a smile at the corners of his mouth.

I took him through the side yard to the back of the house. Not the thing to do with company, but I didn't think Mother or Grace would look too kindly on the dirt we'd trek through the parlor. We washed up a bit at the well, but even I could see it would take a lot more than cold well water to get that boy clean. I only hoped Mother wouldn't insist he take a bath.

I opened the back door. Mother and Grace were in the kitchen preparing the meal. The twins were nowhere in sight, probably still glued to the front window watching the spectacle in the street.

"I'm home, and I've brought a guest," I said.

Abel stepped up beside me. He seemed suddenly shy now that there were womenfolk around.

"This is Abel Hoke. A drummer from Tennessee."

Grace stared at him openmouthed. I almost busted out laughing at the sight. If only Mrs. Eyster could have seen her.

Mother covered her surprise by smoothing her apron.

Abel snatched the hat off his head. I had thought his hair was dirt brown, but I could see that under the cap it was blond like mine. It took a powerful lot of dirt to change a man's hair color.

"Welcome, Abel," Mother said. "I hope you don't mind a simple supper tonight. We've been in quite the uproar today."

"No, ma'am," Abel told her turning his cap

around and around. "It's been some time since I've had more than camp cooking. I'm sure everything will be delicious."

"Please take your things off and sit," Mother said, waving toward the table. "You must be tired from marching."

Abel looked even skinnier without his drum and haversack. He skirted the room so that the women wouldn't get a look at him from behind, and sat at the table. A Rebel. At our supper table.

The twins were all googly-eyed and giggly, as if Abel were a circus freak.

He smiled at them and told them they could play his drum. Soon they were all good friends.

Grace, after her initial shock, was quiet. She clamped her lips together when she got a look at Abel's feet. Her eyes kept darting to the giant hole in his shirt, hidden at first by the drum, and the dirt-covered skin underneath.

Mother set another place and put the meal on the table. Cold ham, bread with apple butter, and boiled beans. Mother said grace, and we passed the food. Abel reminded me of a horse at a Fourth of July race, straining for the starter gun to go off. He picked up a piece of ham in one hand and a slice of bread in the other and rammed them into his mouth. He kept his head down and shoveled it in like he hadn't seen food in a week. He didn't look up until his plate was empty.

Suddenly he noticed the rest of us were using forks. His face turned a deep shade of red.

"I'm sorry, ma'am," he said. "I've been among soldiers too long."

Mother patted his hand. "I'm glad to see a boy with such a healthy appetite," she said calmly, filling his plate with seconds of everything.

This time, Abel used his fork.

"Did you say you were from Tennessee?" Mother asked.

"Yes, ma'am, from the western part of the state."

"Your mother must be missing you," Mother said.

"I miss her, too," Abel answered. "Especially now." He eyed the twins. "I've got sisters and a little brother at home."

I didn't want to hear about that all over again, and there was no telling what Mother would do when she heard about Abel's daddy. I changed the subject. "Abel joined up when he was *ten*," I said.

"Yes, ma'am," Abel nodded. "With my daddy."

"You been in many battles?" I asked.

Abel shrugged. "Enough."

"You ever drummed the order to charge?"

"I'll not have battle talk at the table," Mother said.

Grace smiled at me in that satisfied way of hers. "When did you see your family last?" she asked.

"Ain't been home for about a year," Abel told her.

Grace's lips twitched with the desire to correct his English. But he was a guest, so she couldn't. Ha! Suddenly I realized she couldn't correct my English, either—not without embarrassing Abel.

"Abel's been marching for days and days, *ain't* that right, Abel?" I said.

Grace's lips twitched even more.

He nodded.

I imagined life on the march. Sleeping under the stars, eating with my hands, saying ain't whenever I had a mind to.

"I *ain't* never been outside of Pennsylvania," I said, drawing a kick from Grace. I tried to kick her back but she moved her legs.

"The country around here sure is pretty, but it doesn't come close to home in my eyes."

Mother kept Abel talking about his home and family for quite some time, making it impossible for me to ask him everything I wanted to know about life on the march.

Abel said he had to find his unit before it got too dark. And I never did get to try out my drumming.

I eyeballed those dirty feet of his, and I couldn't let him leave just yet.

"Wait!" I bolted up the stairs and dove under my bed, locating my second pair of shoes—my best. I had been turning over this idea in my mind ever since I saw that my feet and Abel's were about the same size. Even though he was the enemy, he was just a boy like me and I didn't want to send him away shoeless. I had two pairs, and he had none. Then I grabbed some trousers. He couldn't march around with his backside hanging out like that. It wasn't proper.

I pushed the shoes and the trousers into his hands before Mother or Grace could stop me.

I half expected Mother to scold me, but her eyes filled with tears and she put her hand on my shoulder. "I think we can find a clean shirt for Abel, too, can't we?" she asked me.

Abel stared at my things as if they were gold.

Then he gave the trousers back. "I'll likely get myself shot if I wear these," he said. "But I sure do appreciate the shoes."

He was right. The trousers were blue. His own unit might shoot him for a Union man in blue.

The next thing I knew mother was tearing apart a pair of Jacob's old trousers, gray ones, and making them Abel-sized on her Singer sewing machine while Grace wrapped some food for his haversack. I got a clean shirt for him and some under things.

Finally, we had him fully outfitted.

Abel grinned proudly. "My captain won't recognize me," he said. He lifted his drum and slipped the strap over his shoulders before stepping out the front door.

"I'm grateful for all you've done for me," he said to all of us. Then he turned to me. "I hope you'll visit me in Tennessee when the war's over. I sure would be proud to introduce you to my mama."

"I will," I said quietly. I wanted to. I suddenly wanted the war to end. For Abel to stay alive and see his mama again.

He stepped into the street. Mother called him back.

"Stay with us," she said, her eyes filling with

tears again. "Stay with us. We'll hide you here until the army's gone. Then we'll find a way to get you home to your mama."

"Much obliged, ma'am," Abel said, nodding in that way he had. "I've got my duty." Then he turned around again and marched down Baltimore Street looking for his unit.

That night the sky was a fiery red. We learned that the Rebels had set fire to the railroad bridge over Rock Creek, along with all our railroad cars and the engine house. We had no railroad anymore. We were completely cut off from Harrisburg and Philadelphia.

Mother made us all stay in her room. The girls slept sideways on Mother's bed, and I had a pile of blankets on the floor.

The events of the day ran through my head when I closed my eyes. I had watched the enemy thunder down the street right in front of me. I nearly got killed by one Rebel and then made friends with another one.

Joe had said I cost him three Negroes. I wondered who got away. I think Father would have been proud of me for what I had done, even though it almost got me killed.

As I drifted off to sleep I wished he was here.

The Rebels were already stirring when I woke up the next morning. By eight o'clock, the prisoners in the Courthouse were paroled and the Rebels marched away. They were headed east, toward York. Before they left, they lowered their Confederate flag and cut down the flagpole, preventing us from raising the Stars and Stripes again.

Folks ventured out into the street, blinking as if the sun had come out after days and days of rain. The town was ours again, and we didn't quite know what to do with it. Then four Union scouts rode into town practically on the heels of the Rebs.

We gathered around them. Folks shouted over one another, telling the scouts all they knew about the size of the Rebel forces and the direction they were headed in.

"They told me they plan to be in this part of the state all summer," Mrs. Buehler said.

"They aim to take Harrisburg," Mr. Pierce added.

"Is the Union army headed this way?" I asked.

The scouts didn't know—or wouldn't say. But they did know the Confederates were on the move. "More of Lee's army is headed into this part of the state," one of them told me.

It seemed clear that there would be a battle sometime soon. I watched the scouts ride out of town and wondered if Abel and his drum would survive.

★ CHAPTER SEVEN ★

Intolerable Suspense

Sunday, June 28, 1863

T hose scouts must have let the Union army know what was what. Just as church services were coming to a close Sunday morning, a blue column of Union cavalry trooped over the Baltimore Street hill and into the square.

They didn't thunder down the street whooping and hollering, trying to scare us and show us who was boss. People didn't feel the need to hide in their houses, either, like they did when the Rebs came. Folks lined the streets cheering.

I was proud to see how strong the soldiers looked, not a bare foot or a rag among them. I saw a couple of men with buckets of water, handing out drinks. I ran and filled our bucket at the well and grabbed a tin cup so I could do the same.

A full colonel with a big mustache leaned down and took the cup from my hand.

"Much obliged, young man," he said.

I beamed at him.

Grace and Mother spread apple butter on as much bread as we had in the house, and the twins stood beside me on the sidewalk handing it out. Others passed out pie and cake. Girls waved handkerchiefs and sang patriotic songs.

Hurrah! Hurrah! Hurrah! Hurrah!
Our country forever.
Our country forever.
Hurrah! Hurrah! Hurrah! Hurrah!
Our country and flag.
Our country and flag.

They got stuck on the chorus. One of the soldiers laughed and asked them to sing the actual verses, but it turned out that none of the girls knew the words. So he filled in with his deep voice:

*Our nation must stand throughout all
future ages,*
　　*Enshrined in our hearts and in history's
pages;*
　　*As bought with the blood of our fathers
we cherish*
　　*And swear to preserve and maintain it,
or perish.*
　　Hurrah! Hurrah! Our Union forever.
　　Hurrah! Hurrah! Our country and flag.

The girls came in again on the chorus, and
when they finished this time everyone cheered!

The Union soldiers spent the night in town,
camped on the same streets the Rebels had slept on.

Even with their presence, I didn't ask to sleep
in my own room that night. I made my nest of
blankets on the floor of Mother's room, while the
girls snuggled up against her in the bed.

The soldiers left after breakfast the next morning.
I was more than a little sad to see them go. What
if the Rebels came back? Would we have to let
them take over the way they did before?

We had no idea what was happening in the

country around us. The town was completely cut off. We had no telegraph. No railroad. From the rooftops, with the aid of field glasses, we knew that the Rebel encampments were growing bigger by the hour.

It was like I didn't know up from down. One minute I was scared. The next I was sure that nothing would happen. Then I found myself wishing for a fight, just so I could see one.

I hoped the Union cavalry would catch the Rebels and give them a sound thrashing. All except Abel that is.

It seemed more and more likely that a battle would be fought. Where and when were the mystery.

The suspense grew intolerable.

Two things happened after dark that night to make us forget our fears, at least for a little while.

The first was that Aunt Bess crept into our yard and knocked on the back door.

Sally and Jane Ann rushed to hug her. I knew she had been rounded up with the other Negroes, but I didn't know who had managed to escape when I made my run at the slave catchers. I also hadn't told Mother about my act, sure that she would find it wild and reckless.

"I just come to thank that boy of yours for saving me from a slow, painful death in the South," she said.

Mother looked from Aunt Bess to me with a confused expression.

"He created one heck of a commotion with those devil Rebs," Aunt Bess explained. "I saw my chance and made my escape. Those monsters would have taken me south for sure. I would have died in slavery."

The twins stared as if I was a war hero. Grace tried to hide the fact that she was impressed. Mother shot me a look that let me know we'd be talking about this later.

I shrugged. "It was nothing," I said, suddenly embarrassed.

"Where've you been since then?" Mother asked Aunt Bess.

"I made my way into the belfry of Christ Lutheran," she said. "Someone told the Rebs I hightailed it up Chambersburg Street. Those fools didn't even look in the church. I stayed in that belfry for two days. I had no food to eat or water to drink, but it was better than being marched down south, and that's the God's truth."

Christ Lutheran Church was right across the

street from where the line of Negroes had been. Aunt Bess must have slipped into the church while I was shouting my crazy Rebel yell.

"You must stay here," Mother said. "We'll find a good hiding place for you if the Confederates come back."

Aunt Bess shook her head. "No, ma'am. I have a place—a good place—and I ain't telling no one where it is. No one's going to find me where I'm going. I aim to stay there until the North is free from all those Southern devils."

We all tried to get her to change her mind. Sally and Jane Ann both started to cry with the drama of it all. Grace wrapped some food and Mother pressed a blanket on the old woman. I could only hope that Aunt Bess was right. That her hiding place would keep her safe until the Rebels were driven out of Pennsylvania.

The other good news swept through town like a sharp, winter wind. A local man had managed to hide a horse from the Confederates. That night he slipped past the Rebel camps and rode down Emmitsburg Road. He came back with welcome news.

"Union forces are near, and they're on their way."

CHAPTER EIGHT

Storybook Knights

Tuesday, June 30, 1863

We didn't wake up to the news that we expected—that Union forces had arrived. Instead, mounted Confederate officers appeared on the crest of Seminary Ridge, overlooking Gettysburg. The news was passed from house to house. Their infantry pickets, the soldiers in front of the main army who watched for the enemy to approach, moved closer to town.

Almost before that news had finished spreading, we heard that a column of Union cavalry was moving northeast along the Emmitsburg Road. It seemed like the two armies were going to meet right here, in the center of town.

The Union cavalry arrived a little before noon. Mother spotted them first from the kitchen window as they passed northwardly along Washington Street. The whole town flocked to see them. Their colors flew before them. Their horses were big and strong, and their swords and bayonets sparkled in the sunshine. They rode along looking like storybook knights.

Once again, folks gave them water and food while the girls sang patriotic songs.

I sat on the top rail of a fence next to Charlie McCurdy and offered them cherries.

This group of soldiers said they planned to stick around some. When they all had passed us and turned west on Chambersburg Street, I jumped to my feet. "Let's go!" I said.

Charlie and I followed them, running behind the horses, along with Albertus McCreary and a bunch of other boys. They rode in the direction of the Seminary—exactly where we had seen the enemy that morning. The Confederates turned tail as soon as they saw our men.

"Cowards," I muttered.

"Traitors," Albertus agreed.

"Southern devils," I added, using Aunt Bess's words for them.

We entertained each other with tales of the whipping they would get at the hands of the Union troops.

The cavalry let us help them set up camp in the fields near Pennsylvania College, and I rode three different horses to water. We told the soldiers all about the Rebel invasion.

"They stood on our flag, and then they broke our flagpole," I told them. "And boy did they smell!"

"And he knows that for sure," Charlie said.

I froze. Did Charlie know about Abel? Was it treason to feed a Confederate, even if he was a boy?

"He ran right up to some Rebels and made them let the Negroes go," Charlie continued. "They almost killed him. It was the bravest thing I ever saw."

Obviously, rumors about my run-in had been exaggerated as they spread through town. Charlie wasn't even there to see it.

"That so, little man?" one of the soldiers asked. "You ready to join up?"

"I only copied their crazy Rebel yell and ran

at them," I said. "A few of the Negroes got away, though."

The soldier chuckled and patted me on the shoulder.

"When you're ready to join up, you ask for Buford's First Cavalry division. We need men like you."

I knew he was teasing, but still it felt good. I'd guessed that Buford was the serious man who kept riding back and forth and looking through his field glasses. Then he climbed to the cupola on top of the Lutheran Seminary and looked out over the land all around us. Once he was satisfied, he sat in front of his tent and talked with some other officers. I wished I knew what they were planning. But when I tried to get close, an aide shooed me away.

The men were building cook fires and preparing for supper. I wished I could spend the night out here with them, eating their camp food and sleeping on the earth. But I knew Mother would be worried. I had to get home.

When I got there, Grace was over at the Pierces'. The girls were all making bouquets of flowers for the soldiers. I snorted when she came in with a basketful of nosegays.

"What in tarnation do soldiers want with flowers," I said. "They're going to a battle, not a tea dance."

Grace stuck her nose in the air and flounced up the stairs. "I'm sure the *men* will appreciate our gift," she said. "A *boy* like you wouldn't understand."

I stuck my tongue out at her back. Which one of us had spent the afternoon with soldiers?

That night the girls bunked with Mother again, but I slept in my own bed. There was a large force of Union soldiers between the enemy and us. Gettysburg was safe.

★ CHAPTER NINE ★

A Dance
with the Enemy

Wednesday morning, July 1, 1863

I raced through my chores Wednesday morning—there were fewer of them with Molasses
hidden away with the Baileys' horses—and ran to
the campground to see if I could help water the
cavalry's horses again.

The air was heavy and thick. It would rain later.
The smell of coffee and horses grew the nearer I
got to camp. The men were finishing breakfast,
putting out fires, and packing their gear. They
were more serious than the night before. Less
willing to talk. I was sorry to see that they were

leaving so soon, but everyone in town thought the Rebels must be marching on Harrisburg. The Union army would never let them take the state capital. They had to set out after the Rebels.

Suddenly we heard a bugle call and the distant *pop, pop, pop* of rifle fire. The soldiers scrambled to fall in.

"The ball is about to begin," one of them said to me as he mounted his horse. "Fancy a dance with the enemy today?"

He rode off before I could answer.

I would have liked to tell him that I was ready. "Give me a drum, and I'll beat the orders. Give me a musket, and I'll fire on the enemy." I saw myself dirty and tired at the end of the day, gathered around a campfire with the other men. We'd laugh about how we drove the Rebels all the way back to Virginia.

Then I remembered how it felt to have a musket pointed at my head. Would I be brave enough to fight? What if I had to point my musket at Abel, or a boy like him?

Someone said we should run to Seminary Ridge to get a look at the fighting. I wondered if I should go home to Mother and the girls, but I wanted to see the battle, too. I promised myself I would only stay a few minutes. No doubt our men would take care of the Rebs in no time.

The ridge was full of men and boys waiting to see the Rebels get a fair drumming from our side. I climbed a tall oak tree in back of the Seminary building. I could see all the action. There were a lot more Rebs than Union men. They had their cannons lined up on Herr's Ridge, ready to fire. The Union cavalry had dismounted and made a line of battle facing them on McPherson's Ridge.

The Rebs advanced, coming nearer, but the Union men made them fight for every inch. Then the Rebel cannons opened fire. Dragons with fiery breath roared and sent shells flying. The air was full of smoke and the smell of saltpeter.

I was sure we were far enough away, but then some of those Rebel shells missed their mark and flew in our direction. One sailed through the air. It sounded like it was coming right at me.

"Watch out!" someone yelled.

I curled my body into a ball and gripped my branch. The sounds of the battle disappeared, and all I heard was the shell whistle as it flew over my head. Limbs cracked. Leaves and branches fell to the ground. Behind me there was a loud thud as the shell hit the earth, followed by an explosion.

I opened my eyes, stunned to be alive. Then I climbed out of that tree so fast I'm not sure I didn't sprout wings and fly. There was a deep gouge in the earth, like a grave. I swallowed hard, thinking that my dead body might have been lying there along with the shell.

I took a deep breath to steady myself and then joined the stampede toward town.

The part of town nearest the battle was all chaos and confusion. People ran here and there, yelling that the town would be shelled. Some had already packed their things and were heading south, away from the fighting. Others went about their daily business with an air of determination. I saw Mr. Broadhead picking beans in his garden.

"Not going to leave any for the Rebels," he said.

I ran down West Middle Street toward Baltimore. Daniel Skelley and some others were on the observatory deck on top of the Fahnestock Brothers store. I thought I should go home to comfort Mother and the girls, but I decided to take one last look at the battle first.

The Union line had been pushed farther back.

I worried the Rebs were winning, but Daniel pointed to the Union soldiers moving over the fields from the Emmitsburg Road in front of Dr. Schmucker's, under cover of Seminary Ridge.

"There's the infantry!" he shouted. "They'll get them!"

I was about to go home when a Union general and his staff rode down Baltimore Street from the south. It was only then that I realized how mixed up this battle was. The Rebels were coming at us from the north of town, and the Union soldiers from the south.

The general stopped at the Courthouse and looked up at the belfry. We thought he would get a better view of the battlefield from our observation deck, so I ran down to the street.

"There's a clear view from the roof, sir," I said. "We can see all the fighting."

"Lead the way," he said.

"It started around eight o'clock this morning," I told him, leading him and a few aides up to the Fahnestock Brothers' third story. We went through the trapdoor and onto the roof. "At first it was just the cavalry on our side, but the infantry joined the fight about an hour ago. There are a lot of Rebs out there, but I know you'll beat them."

The general greeted everyone with a nod but said nothing more. He used field glasses to watch the battle and survey the land around town. I stood at the ready, hoping he would have more questions for me.

Seeing things through a stranger's eyes sure can change your view. I saw that our Diamond was in the center of everything. There were roads all around town like spokes on a wheel, and every single one of them headed straight for the center of Gettysburg. No wonder both armies found us.

The general pointed out Cemetery Hill to his aides. It was back where they had come from. Was he already planning a retreat? I had no time to ask the question. A scout pounded down West Middle Street at full gallop, shouting for General Howard.

The general with us called out that he was Howard.

"General Reynolds is dead," the scout yelled. "You are wanted on the battlefield immediately."

I thought about Abel's simple words. "Dead. Shiloh."

Did General Reynolds have children? Would they have to say, "Dead. Gettysburg," when someone asked about their father?

All of sudden I was glad my father wasn't a soldier, but safe in an army hospital treating the injured. I was glad Jacob was a prisoner and not in the middle of a battle.

General Howard gave instructions to one of his aides to ride back and hurry the rest of the infantry along, leaving some men behind to occupy and fortify Cemetery Hill. Then, in an instant, he was galloping toward the fighting.

About ten thirty, more infantry soldiers marched down Washington Street, heading for the battle. I had forgotten all about going home. Instead I perched on the plank fence around Mrs. Eyster's Young Ladies Seminary to cheer them on.

Their uniforms were the thickest kind of wool. Most men had wool blankets and knapsacks belted to their backs. Cartridge boxes and canteens hung over their shoulders. They had been caught in the rain and dripped water and sweat in the hot July weather.

They marched on the double-quick through rows of townspeople handing them cake and bread with apple butter and water. The men would grab a tin cup, drink, and fling it back as they ran.

They didn't have the easy confidence of the cavalry from the day before. These men were headed into battle. We could hear the shells thundering, the muskets popping. Some of these men would die today. They knew it. Now I did, too.

Officers urged the people to stop feeding them—we were slowing the soldiers down—but no one wanted to send them into battle without food and water and shouts of encouragement. It was the only thing we could do.

A military band had set up on the Diamond to play "The Star-Spangled Banner" and other patriotic airs. There was a chorus of bullets and shells behind them. Wounded men limped through the streets. I saw one Union soldier cleaning his hand in a horse trough. A bullet had gone clean through his flesh.

"There are enough soldiers here to whip all the Rebs in the South," Albertus McCreary yelled.

My stomach was beginning to fill with dread, but I pretended to share his excitement. "I bet the war ends today," I said. "And we'll win it!"

I saw a column of Confederates being marched through town under a Union guard. Prisoners! I thought the Union must be winning. Abel's face flashed across my mind for a moment, and then I shook him off. The Union and Abel couldn't both win this battle, and I was for the Union. Abel would have to lose with the rest of the Rebels.

I cheered and cheered until my voice was hoarse and my throat sore. I realized I had better head on home and make sure Mother was all right.

Grace and I reached the kitchen door at the same time. She carried an empty basket.

"I hope you gave those soldiers nourishment instead of nosegays," I told her.

She grabbed my ear and dragged me into the kitchen. "You've had Mother worried sick," she said.

I shrugged her off. What did she know? "I was helping a general," I told her. "A Union general," I said again, waiting for a reaction.

She ignored me. Only set down her basket and walked into the parlor.

I followed her.

Mother was talking with Mrs. Shriver and Tillie Pierce. The noise from exploding shells had grown considerably now that the infantry was in the fight. The twins jumped with each boom. China clattered in the cabinet. Jacob's picture fell from the wall, and the glass in the frame shattered.

Mother went white. The twins clung to her and started to cry. Grace's lips trembled.

"Don't you see?" Mrs. Shriver said, wringing her hands. "If we don't leave here, we'll all be killed."

★ CHAPTER TEN ★

A Family Separated

Wednesday afternoon, July 1, 1863

Mother picked up the frame and slipped it into her apron. "I don't believe the Union will let them take the town," she said.

"The children, then," Mrs. Shriver said. "Let me take them with me."

"Take them where?" Grace asked.

"Mrs. Shriver is taking her children to her parents' farm until the battle is over," Mother said calmly. "Tillie is going with them."

I knew the Weikert farm. It was about three miles away, out by the hills called the Round Tops. We picnicked there sometimes in the summer, and cooled ourselves in Rock Creek nearby. It was far from the fighting.

Was Mother going to send us away? Already Father and Jacob were far from home; would Mother further divide us? Stay here by herself with a battle waging outside? I couldn't let her.

"I'm not going," I said. "I'll stay with you. Send the girls away."

Mother eyed me steadily for a moment, and then turned to Grace. "I want you to take the twins and go with Mrs. Shriver," Mother said. "You'll be safer there."

Grace started to object, but Mother shushed her. "It will give me peace of mind to know that you're away from all this."

I steeled myself for a battle of my own.

Mother surprised me. "Will can stay here with me. I'd appreciate the company."

I pushed my shoulders back and stood tall, proud to be singled out to stay. I told myself that Grace had to leave town just when things were getting exciting. That I wanted to be in the middle of all the action.

After a short whispered exchange with Tillie, Grace ran upstairs. She clattered back down with her best dress in her arms.

"What in the world?" I blurted. Where did she think she was going, to a church social?

Grace ignored me. She went out front and opened the cellar doors. A minute later, she came back empty-handed. "I'll not have my best things ruined," she said.

"I'll see you for supper tonight, or in time for breakfast tomorrow. This battle will be over before we know it," Mother told the twins, giving them a hug. "You mind Grace."

Sally and Jane Ann held hands and sniffled a bit, but they seemed to enjoy the idea of an adventure. It helped that they adored Tillie, the prettiest girl in town, and often played with the Shriver children.

Mother and I stood on the doorstep and watched them go. First Jacob, then Father, and now Grace and the twins.

I squeezed Mother's hand. "They'll be back before I even have a chance to miss them," I told her. "And Grace will be bossier than ever."

Mother started to reply, then gasped and gripped my arm. I turned my head in the direction of her stare. A wagon pulled up in front of the Courthouse. What appeared to be a dead man lay in the back. There were a few wounded soldiers with him. Those who could walk helped the others inside.

"Go with the girls, Will," Mother said.

Part of me wanted to run after them as fast as I could, to get away from these dead and wounded men. But I couldn't leave Mother there alone. "You just said I could stay!"

"Walk with them as far as the cemetery," she said. "Then I'll know that they're safely away."

I had to make sure that this wasn't part of a secret plan between Mother and Grace. That Grace wouldn't force me to stay with her once I was out of town.

"I'm coming back," I said firmly.

Mother nodded. "I'll be in the Courthouse," she said. "Those men will need nurses. Let me know that the girls are safe, and that you are, too."

Mother and I left the house together. She turned in the direction of the Courthouse to help the wounded. I went the other way.

I caught up with Mrs. Shriver and the others quickly. My plan was to take my leave of them when we reached the cemetery. But Cemetery Hill was full of Union soldiers preparing their cannon to fire, and I thought I'd best see them farther along.

"Get yourself into a cellar," one of the soldiers told us. "You're in danger!"

Grace tried to talk Mrs. Shriver into stopping at the cemetery's gatehouse and taking refuge there, but Mrs. Shriver flat out refused. She was determined to make it to her parents' farm.

We could see the battle on Seminary Ridge. Shells burst in the air and on land. Whenever the smoke lifted we saw soldiers running all around and the smaller puffs of rifle fire. The noise was loud enough to set my ears to ringing.

Taneytown Road was full of Union soldiers heading for the fight. I could not see the end of the line in either direction.

Between the morning's rain and the tramping of thousands and thousands of boots, the road had turned into a thick muck up to our ankles. The twins could not walk in it. Grace and I each lifted one onto our backs and struggled forward while Tillie and Mrs. Shriver helped her two young ones.

An ambulance wagon passed. Sally hid her face in my shoulder so as not to see the man in the back. Grace's eyes were fixed in front of her. Jane Ann stared, her mouth a perfect O of surprise.

The man wore a crimson rose on his blue coat.

It wasn't a flower. It was blood. I stared right into his eyes, waiting for them to blink. They did not. He was dead.

Grace stumbled to her knees, exhausted. We only had gone halfway. Mrs. Shriver and Tillie looked as worn out as I felt. The young ones were utterly done in. Too done in to make it all the way to the Weikert farm. But going back would take just as long as going forward. I did not know what to do.

I spotted a farmhouse just ahead. "Let's stop there for a rest," I said. I wished the whole group of them would stay there until the battle was over, but I didn't think Mrs. Shriver would be willing.

"The Leisters'," Mrs. Shriver said. "Yes, let's stop for some water."

The soldiers had drunk the well dry. The people of the house had fled, and a Union general was using it as his headquarters. The place was full of soldiers, some of them wounded.

I explained our predicament to one of the general's aides. "I have to get these women and children about a mile and a half down the Taneytown Road. Can you help us?"

To my great relief, he agreed to try. We waited

under the shade of a sycamore tree while he saw what he could do.

He waved us to the front of the house a few minutes later. We struggled through the mud to reach him. Grace stepped right out of one of her shoes, and I had to dig it out of the muck for her.

"I've found a wagon," the soldier said when we finally reached him. "This farmer has agreed to take you the rest of the way."

Grace eyed the wagon with concern. It was already quite full of household goods, and the driver was in a hurry to get himself and his wife away from the battle as quickly as possible. Mrs. Shriver and the girls had to crush themselves between the family's treasures. The wheels sunk up to their hubs once they settled. It would take a long time to reach their destination.

Sally wailed as they drove off. "Will! I want Will!"

I felt like I had been punched in the gut. I knew she would forget all about me in a minute, but still it pained me to hear the fear and sadness in her cry. She and Jane Ann did not understand. Each day they looked for Father to come home, no matter how many times we told them he would be away for some time. They didn't remember Jacob at all. They were just three when he left.

I watched as they drove off, listening to Sally's cries. I don't know why I could hear her above the sounds of battle. Or maybe I just imagined that I could.

More and more soldiers tramped toward them and me. When they came to the wagon they parted around it and then closed up again, like water around a rock in a river.

I stood there for a long time, telling myself that I could still see the wagon. But I couldn't really. I finally turned and headed back toward town. I took to the fields as much as possible to avoid the mud, and my way home was a great deal quicker without the children.

When I reached the edge of town, artillery caissons and wagons were coming at me at the gallop. A trickle of Union men ran behind them. At the top of Baltimore Street hill I could see even more men running, some of them throwing off their guns and their knapsacks as they ran to lighten their load. Others carried wounded on their backs.

An officer galloped past, shouting, "Women and children to the cellars. The Rebels will shell the town!"

I grabbed a man's arm. "You're retreating?" I asked him.

"Simply changing fronts," he said.

The wild mob that ran toward me was not changing fronts. They were retreating, leaving us in the hands of the enemy.

I screamed at them to stop. No one heard. No one cared. A man tried to scale a fence into the alley and then gave up. He shoved his way into the throng on the street again. For a moment, I saw his eyes. They were desperate, wild. What had they seen that he would act so?

What was going to happen to Mother? To me?

The officer wheeled his horse around and shouted again, loud enough for everyone to hear. "All you good people, go down into your cellars or you will be killed."

★ CHAPTER ELEVEN ★

"To your cellar!"

I expected to find Mother at the Courthouse, but she had already returned home. She was on the doorstep, giving water to the retreating men. I nodded to let her know that the girls were safe. Her eyes filled with tears and she nodded back. There was too much uproar around us to talk.

I was glad about that. What was there to say? Our men were retreating. Running.

It was better not to think about it, to concentrate on small tasks like making my way to Mother, dipping a cup into the bucket.

Even so, I couldn't help but see exhausted soldiers drop out of the rushing throng, slip into alleys and yards and houses. Their clothes and skin were black with dirt and gunpowder. Streams of sweat poured down their faces. Many were wounded.

The Union forces were in complete disorder, running helter-skelter. There were more men on Baltimore Street than I had ever seen. I could have stepped my way across the street on their heads without ever touching ground. A couple of them ran into our side yard, only to find a dead end at our fence. They ran out again and pushed their way back into the blue wave that surged past.

The men grabbed for the water and urged us to safety at the same time. "To your cellar!"

I looked up and saw soldiers in gray about a half block away. They struggled in hand-to-hand fighting with some of our men.

"We've got to go," I said, grabbing mother's arm. I fought to appear calm, but my hands were shaking as I struggled to open the cellar door.

Mother left the water bucket and helped me. A wounded man limped in behind us and pulled the doors closed. He dropped to his knees on the dirt floor, panting. One of his arms was covered in blood.

My heart raced. I stood on my toes to peer out the cellar window while Mother tried to help him. We had no water to give him, or bandages for his wounds. There was fighting all around the house, but mostly blue legs still.

A cannon suddenly stopped on the street right in front of me. The Union men fired down Baltimore Street toward the Diamond, trying to stop the Confederate advance. The noise and the dust were terrific, but one artillery shell couldn't hold off the whole Rebel army. In a few minutes, gray uniforms outnumbered the blue ones around our house.

"Shoot that man going over the fence!" one of them yelled.

There was a loud bang and then a scream.

"Got 'em!"

I closed my eyes and slumped against the wall, swallowing hard to hold the contents of my stomach down. This was not the battle of my daydreams. I had not imagined the sharp, hot smell of blood mixed with saltpeter. I had not imagined men running, scared. I had not imagined joy in the killing. The words "Got 'em" echoed in my ears.

I had not imagined the fear, sharp and metallic in my mouth.

Things quieted down and I peered out the window again. There was no blue anymore. Only gray.

Seconds later, a Southern voice warned his comrades not to drink the "wawtah" we had left for the soldiers in front of our house.

"Bet it's poisoned," he said. "Wouldn't be a bit surprised if these Yankee devils poisoned their wells, too."

Mother pursed her lips at the thought. "No Gettysburg woman would do such a thing," she muttered.

Her calmness amazed me. "Will they kill us?" I asked the Union soldier.

He shook his head with a groan. "But they will me. Where can I hide?"

We quickly pulled some barrels into the corner, leaving just enough room for him to crouch behind them. He handed Mother a diary and asked her to keep it for him.

"My name and address are on the flyleaf," he told her. "Please send it to my wife, if—"

The cellar doors burst opened. Mother slipped

the diary into her apron's pocket. I dropped an empty crate on top of the Union man. Three Confederates stomped down the stairs.

"Any Yankees down here?" the first one asked.

Mother pushed me behind her. "My son and I are both Yankees," she told him.

"I mean soldiers," he spat. His gun was trained on us.

We both shook our heads no. I held my breath. What if they looked behind us? Would all three of us be shot?

Then I saw it. There was blood on the floor. A bright red stain only just beginning to seep into the dirt. I tried not to look at it, sure that I would draw it to the Rebels' attention. Only I couldn't control my eyes. They kept flicking to the stain, and away again.

Two of the Rebels walked around the cellar, poking into barrels. One of them stabbed his bayonet into the ash barrel. He found our hidden ham.

"You won't mind if we search upstairs," the first one said.

It wasn't a question. It was an order.

"Of course not," Mother said. "Let's all go upstairs. I can cook some of that ham for you." She took the first soldier by the arm and led him toward the stairs like he was the preacher come for Sunday dinner.

The other two followed, grabbing all the canned goods they could carry. I brought up the rear.

"My son can probably scare up some beans from the garden if they haven't been trampled. And I have some potatoes in the kitchen," Mother said.

The idea of home-cooked food must have distracted them. They followed her up to the street without searching the cellar. The wounded soldier remained safely hidden. They never saw the blood on the floor.

Upstairs, we found two Union men hiding in the kitchen. One Reb stayed behind to guard them while the others searched the bedrooms. I followed. They found two more Union men under the beds. And then one in the garret.

The Rebels took their weapons and marched their prisoners downstairs into the kitchen. One had been shot in the arm.

"I thought you said there were no Yankee soldiers here," the Rebel in charge said suspiciously.

Mother's eyes widened. "They must have come

into the house while we were in the cellar. I had no knowledge of them."

"Well, they're prisoners now," the Reb told her. He picked up the ham. "We'll be getting them out of your way."

"Surely you can all have a meal first," Mother said.

The next thing I knew, five Union prisoners and three Rebel guards were sitting around our table trading stories and jokes while Mother peeled potatoes. With Abel it had been hard enough, but this I didn't understand at all. They had been shooting each other just ten minutes before. Now they acted like old friends.

"Will, go outside and get me another bucket of water from the well," Mother said. "And see if there are any beans worth picking."

I did as I was told. At some point the fighting ended and a strange quiet settled over the town. I couldn't imagine the battle was over for good. If General Howard was true to his words of this morning, then the Union army would be setting themselves up on Cemetery Hill just outside of town. The two armies were only taking a breather, and Gettysburg was trapped right in the middle of them.

The Rebels tore down fences and built barricades in the street, but for now there was no more shooting, no more cannon fire.

At least Grace and the twins were safe, I thought. If Father were here, he would be treating the wounded. Jacob would do whatever he could to make sure Mother was unharmed. I had to try to do the same.

I found enough beans to fill a small bowl. Then I set about getting the water.

That's when I heard a noise that didn't fit in with the other sounds around me. I stood still for a minute, listening. It seemed to come from the carriage house. I opened the door and let my eyes adjust to the dark.

A Union soldier crouched behind Father's carriage, holding his side. "Help me," he said.

I looked over my shoulder to see if anyone was watching. "Are you wounded?" I whispered.

"Just a scratch," he answered. "I have to get back to the Union lines."

Our house, our street, our whole town was in Confederate hands. "We're surrounded," I whispered. "The house is full of Rebs, so is the street."

"I have urgent communications for General Meade," the soldier said.

I was too stunned to answer. General Meade—
he was the one in charge of the whole dang Union
army! Took over for Fighting Joe Hooker just a few
days ago. I read it in the newspaper.

"I must get to General Meade," he said again.

"The Rebs have the town," I said. "The Union
retreated."

"There has to be a way to get across the lines," he
said.

"I don't know," I told him. "I don't know how."

He wouldn't take no for an answer. "After dark,"
he said. "Help me. Or go in my place."

★ CHAPTER TWELVE ★

A Risky Plan

Wednesday evening, July 1, 1863

Go in his place? The words were still hanging in the air when I heard Mother call out to me.

"Will, I need that water," she said.

I jumped, hitting my head on the doorway of the carriage house. "Coming!" I said. I turned back to the soldier. "I'll come back," I told him. "I'll try to bring you some food."

"I don't need food," he said in a harsh whisper. "I need to get to General Meade!"

With each step back to the house, I expected to be shot. I set down the bucket in the kitchen with shaking hands. Mother cupped my chin and looked into my eyes. I gave my head a small shake so she would know not to ask.

"Will," she said brightly, "why don't you take down the names and addresses of these men so we can let their families know that they are alive and well, even though they are prisoners."

It was a Southern lady who had written to us of Jacob. His captain only knew that he was missing. I was grateful to do the same service for other Union men.

I wasn't grateful to be entertaining Rebels. These fellows weren't anything like Abel. They were in high spirits over the day's victory and seemed to take delight in taunting us.

"How do you like this way of our coming back into the Union?" one of them asked Mother.

"I'd rather your return was peaceful," she answered calmly.

"Your Mr. Lincoln wouldn't let us leave the Union in peace," he said. "So we've come back in war. It was the North that started this struggle, not the South."

One of the Union men, Adam Schurz from Wisconsin, began to argue about who had really started the war, but I couldn't listen. How would

I get the soldier in the carriage house across enemy lines?

I turned the problem over and over in my mind. I did not see how I could do it, but what if the communications he spoke of would turn this battle? What if they meant the difference between a Union defeat and a Union victory?

His words echoed in my mind. "Help me. Or go in my place."

I could almost see it. I'd sneak past the Confederate guards, creeping from doorway to doorway and slithering in the grass. As soon as I reached Union lines, I'd let them know how important my mission was.

But the day's events wove their way into my imaginings. Instead of hearing the thanks of a grateful General Meade, I heard the loud report of a sharpshooter's rifle.

I screamed while a Rebel soldier yelled, "Got 'em!"

Mother put a bowl of steaming potatoes into my hands, drawing me out of my nightmarish fantasy. I couldn't go in the Union soldier's place. Nor did I want to.

I set the potatoes on the table, next to a plate of sliced ham. If it was possible to get across the

Confederate lines, wouldn't the soldier in the carriage house already be on his way? How would I do it, if he couldn't?

The Rebel in charge was still trying to belittle the prisoners at our supper table. "We've taken Baltimore and Harrisburg," he said. "Washington is next. The war will end any day now."

I swallowed hard. Was the South really going to win the war?

"You're spinning tales," one of the Union men answered. "Robert E. Lee's entire army is right here," he said. "The South doesn't have enough men to take all those cities."

That started another debate. I hoped that Union man was right. Even so, I couldn't listen anymore. I walked into the parlor and opened the front door to take a breath.

The Rebs had built a barricade right in front of our house. They had stacked their guns and were cooking and relaxing. I couldn't see the Union lines. Rebels stretched up Baltimore Street as far as I could see.

Across the street, six-year-old Mary McLean leaned out a second-story window and sang at the top of her lungs. "Hang Jeff Davis on a sour apple tree!"

Someone snatched her into the house and slammed the window closed.

I held my breath and waited for the soldiers to fire on her house. Jefferson Davis was the President of the Confederate States. Rebels wouldn't take kindly to songs about him being hanged. The soldiers under the window only laughed and launched into a loud round of "Dixie."

I scanned the street for Abel. If he was in town, I thought he would make his way to our house. But what could he do? I certainly couldn't tell him about the soldier in the carriage house. About the important papers for General Meade. He was the enemy. His duty would be to turn the soldier in, and me for hiding him.

I wished Father were here, or Jacob, or even Grace. I felt frozen despite the heat. Rebels were all around the house. That Union officer would be arrested or shot before he took a step. General Meade would never get his urgent communications.

It would be dark soon. I finally had my chance to join the war. To do my part for the Union, and I was afraid. All I wanted to do was curl up in the cellar with that other soldier and hide.

Some Rebels approached the house. One carried a man on his back. The other held his arm as if he was afraid it would fall off.

"A doctor lives here?" they asked.

"Yes," I said, "but he's not here."

Mother came up behind me. "The Courthouse is being used as a hospital," she said. "And the Presbyterian Church."

"They're both full up," the soldier told her. "Every church, every building in town is full up with wounded."

Mother pulled me out of the doorway so that they could come in. "Bring them into the parlor," she said.

The man being carried moaned something awful when they laid him on the settee. His chest and belly were covered in blood. The other—the one with the wounded arm—dropped into a chair. He could barely sit upright.

"Will, get me some more water," Mother said. "We're going to need it."

The other Rebels came out of the kitchen then, with their prisoners.

"Do you have a red flag to hang from the house," their leader asked.

"Red flag?"

"So the sharpshooters will know this is a hospital," he explained.

"If my house is to be a hospital, then perhaps you'll leave those three gentlemen here," Mother said, pointing to some of the Union men. "They're wounded."

With that, our house became a hospital. Mother hung Grace's red shawl from an upstairs window, and three of the Union prisoners got to stay with us instead of going to prison. I was sorry for the other two. Maybe the Rebs would parole them when the battle ended instead of marching them down south.

"I'll need lots of water," Mother told me. "See if you can find me something to use for bandages."

I headed to the back of the house to get more water from the well. On my way through the kitchen, I shoved a piece of bread into my pocket for the soldier in the carriage house. I would have to tell him there was nothing I could do. There were too many Rebs around. If his papers made the difference between victory and defeat, I guess the defeat would rest on my shoulders.

I was filling the bucket when an idea started to form in the back of my mind. I thought of all the times Father had set out in the dark to help some-one who had taken sick. It seemed like he was al-ways going off in the night.

That's when it hit me. If the soldier was a sur-geon, Union or Reb, he could move around in the dark. Go from place to place. Tend the wounded.

Father had left a medical kit behind. What if the soldier carried it and pretended to be a doc-tor? Would he be able to get across enemy lines?

I set my bucket down and looked all around. No one appeared to be watching me. I crept into the carriage house to share my plan.

★ CHAPTER THIRTEEN ★

White Flags

I whispered my plan in the dark while the soldier wolfed down the bread. He was still crouched behind the carriage.

"I'll need a green sash," he said.

"Green sash?"

"A surgeon's sash," he told me.

I didn't think we had such a thing.

"It might be safer for me to wear one of your father's suits. Pretend I'm him," he said. "Can you bring one to me?"

"I'll try to get one out of the house. There are Rebs inside. Wounded ones."

He crept forward and gripped my arm. "Do what you can," he said. "You'll have to come with me. Show me the way. Say you're my son."

I gasped, much too loudly, and then looked around to see if anyone was close enough to hear. I thought my plan would be enough to keep me at home, but he still wanted me to go with him. My heart was drumming in my ears. I could tell this man was used to giving orders. But I wasn't a soldier. I was scared. And I was probably putting Mother in danger by helping him.

I could just leave him here, I thought. Go back to the house. Never bring him the suit, the medical kit. Help Mother with the wounded. Put him out of my mind. He could find his own way to the Union lines.

It was like he could read my thoughts.

"I'm counting on you, son," he said.

I nodded and slunk back into the yard, sure that I would be shot at any moment. I picked up the bucket and crept in the back door. I realized my legs were shaking when I collapsed on the floor. Sweat dripped down my face, or maybe it was tears. I was too mixed up to know.

The tramp of the guards outside reminded me that we were prisoners. My breath came in quick gasps and I couldn't seem to calm it. Finally, I focused on a piece of crockery on a shelf. My thoughts and my breathing slowed.

The kitchen was dark. Sometime during the day the gasworks had been shut down.

Mother came in with a candle and found me. "Are you hurt?" she asked, rushing over to check my arms and my legs.

"No. Not hurt," I told her. "It's something else."

Mother sat on the floor with me while I whispered my story. Her eyes were wide and frightened in the candlelight. I told her everything in one big rush.

Mother looked as stunned as I felt. It was clear she had to think on it a bit. "I'll just take this into the other room," she said, picking up the bucket. "The men are asking for water."

"He wants me to go with him," I blurted. "To lead the way. Says he needs help getting across the lines."

Mother dropped the bucket. Water sloshed onto the floor. "You're just a boy," she said.

"What if the papers he's carrying can make a difference in the battle? What if they'll help the Union to win?" I asked. "Help Jacob to come home."

One of the Union men came into the kitchen

then, looking for us. Mother asked him if surgeons and their assistants were generally safe from enemy fire.

He didn't ask why she needed that information. "Surgeons and drummers often take to the battlefield after dark, searching for the wounded. Carrying them off the field. He waves a white flag if need be. Folks generally don't shoot. Generally, not always."

Then he picked up the water bucket. "I'll take this into the parlor so that you can be alone for a moment."

"I guess I should go with him," I said reluctantly.

Her eyes filled with tears. She was quiet for a long moment.

I wanted her to refuse her permission, and I wanted her to grant it at the same time. Too many feelings battled for attention in my body. Fear. Shame about being afraid. Anger at the Union officer. And even a little excitement about the idea of becoming the hero I was in my daydreams. Fear seemed to be the strongest, though.

"Jacob would do it," I said. I knew, when I said it, that it was true. "I can help him find his way, and then come back."

"You won't make that journey twice," Mother

said finally. "Find the girls at the Weikert farm and wait out the battle there. It will be safer."

"What about you?" I asked. "If I don't come back, won't the Rebels arrest you? Or shell the house?"

"Those Rebels are too wounded to notice. Two of our Union boys are hardly hurt at all. They can help me with the others."

She pulled me into her arms. We sat mashed together on the kitchen floor. Then Mother got to her feet. "I'll see about getting one of your father's suits."

I leaned back against the wall, closed my eyes, and said a silent prayer. If Mary McLean was brave enough to face the Rebels with her song, I could summon the courage to wave a white flag and pretend the man in the carriage house was my father.

I heard mother walking through the parlor. "One of our neighbors is in need of cloth for bandages," she said. "I'll be right back to check on you boys."

She came into the kitchen with a bundle. "There is no shame in telling him no," she said.

"I'm going," I said. My voice wavered.

"There are two white cloths in there," she told

me. "If that man out there does anything foolish, you leave him to his fate," she said fiercely. "You keep yourself safe."

I promised that I would.

"What's his name?" she asked.

"I don't know."

"I'll need his name before you leave," she said. "I'll not send my boy out into the night without knowing the name of the man he's risking his life for."

I slipped outside with the bundle and brought it to him.

"What's your name?" I whispered.

"My name?"

"My mother requires your name."

"Colonel William Braxton," he said. "I'm one of General Meade's aides."

"I'll be back," I told him.

Mother waited by the back door. Her face looked drawn and tired. I whispered the colonel's name. She nodded and pulled me into another hug before placing a kiss on my forehead. She handed me Father's medical chest.

"I won't watch you leave," she said. "But I'll be watching for you to come home when the battle's over."

I nodded, then waited until she was in the parlor before I slipped outside again. The colonel was standing just inside the carriage house. He held his uniform.

"Bury this," he ordered. "If the Confederates find it there will be trouble."

I knelt in the garden and pretended to be searching for something among the trampled ruins while I dug. As soon as I judged the hole deep enough, I went back to the door of the carriage house.

He handed me his uniform. I pointed to his rifle and his saber. "I'll need those, too," I said. "Surgeons have no call for them."

Reluctantly, he handed them over. I dropped them on top of the uniform and pushed the dirt back on top. I hoped my work wouldn't be obvious in the light of day.

When I stood and brushed the dirt off my trousers, he stepped out of the carriage house. Father's suit was too short in the legs, but the jacket fit the colonel okay.

It was time to begin our journey.

★ CHAPTER FOURTEEN ★

Dr. Edmonds

I tried to ignore the pops and whistles of sharp-shooter bullets as I pushed aside the loose board in our fence and led the colonel into the alley and toward Washington Street.

"What's my name?" the colonel whispered.

"Doctor Joseph Edmonds," I whispered back.

I took a deep breath and tried to steady my quaking knees. Washington Street was full of Rebel soldiers. Some were sleeping with their rifles in their hands, some were singing, others were just staring into the night. A few glanced at the colonel's medical kit, visible in the glow of their campfires, and looked away. Perhaps this would be easier than I thought.

When we reached South Street, I deemed it best that we head back to Baltimore. It was a more direct route to the cemetery. I tripped over someone and started to apologize, then realized, by the stillness of him, that he was dead. I shivered, despite the heat.

A Rebel guard stopped us on the corner of Baltimore Street. He raised his pistol and pointed it at the colonel.

"I'm Dr. Edmonds," the colonel said.

It was the first time I heard his full voice. We had been whispering up until that time. It was a strong, confident baritone.

Even so, the Reb eyed him suspiciously. "There are plenty of hospitals that way," he said, pointing toward the Courthouse.

The colonel was as cool as a steel knife. "We were ordered to attend a wounded officer up the street a ways." He put a hand on my shoulder. "This is my son. He's going to assist me."

"Where?" the Reb asked.

The colonel hesitated. Of course he didn't know. He didn't know the town. I had to speak up.

"At the Rupp house," I said, nodding in that direction. "Just past the tannery." My voice quivered a bit, but not too badly.

"A Confederate officer," the colonel added. "Very seriously wounded. He can't be moved."

I waited for the Reb to pull the trigger. My legs stiffened as if all on their own they had decided to run. I gritted my teeth and dug my heels into the ground so I could stand still.

The Reb let us pass.

"What's past the Rupp house?" the colonel whispered.

"Snider's Wagon Hotel," I whispered back.

We were stopped by several guards, but the colonel gave the same story each time. The Rebs appeared to be in pretty high spirits. They had won the day and were unconcerned about the possibility of a spy in their midst.

One asked us to stop and tend his fellow soldier.

The colonel knelt and looked at the gash in the man's leg. I held my breath and got ready to run. Did he know about doctoring, or would he give us away?

"There's a very badly wounded officer up ahead," he said gently. "This'll wait until I can get back to you." He patted the soldier on the arm. "You'll be fine, son."

"Much obliged, Doc," the Rebel said.

My breath came out in one big rush. I never would have guessed the colonel was lying.

Finally, we reached the Rebel pickets—the soldiers closest to the Union lines. They were just about even with the Rupp house. I knew there had to be Union pickets not too far ahead. I pulled the handkerchief out of my pocket and raised it over my head. The moon was full. I told myself the white cloth would be visible.

"Where do you think y'all are going?" a gruff voice demanded.

The colonel put a hand on my shoulder again. "I'm Dr. Edmonds. There's a man ahead in the Wagon Hotel who needs doctoring. His courier came to the Courthouse a little while ago. Said it was urgent."

"Where's the courier now?" The Reb placed his hand on his pistol.

The colonel pretended not to notice. He shrugged. "Ran on ahead while I was restocking my medical kit." He held the wooden box up as proof.

"Why didn't I see him?"

The colonel shrugged again. "Slipped by unnoticed I expect."

Anger flashed in the Rebel's eyes.

"He's one of yours," the colonel said quickly. "So is the wounded man. An officer. One of Lee's men, I think."

My eyes darted from the pistol to the Reb's face and back again. A sharpshooter's bullet sailed over our heads toward the Union's lines. I jumped.

"Why is there a boy with you?" the Rebel demanded.

"My son," the colonel said calmly. "He's been assisting me."

"Does your son know that the Wagon Hotel is in the Bluebellies' hands?" the Rebel asked. His voice was full of sarcasm.

"I have no enemies," the colonel said. "I'll treat any man who is wounded and needs my care."

The Reb said nothing.

"Perhaps the officer is a prisoner," the colonel said sternly. "This is a life-and-death matter. You must let us go to him."

The man's hand tightened around his pistol.

Then another voice spoke up, coming to us out

of the dark. "That's the doctor's son," it said. "I seen him the other day."

It was too dark for me to see that funny little nod of his, but I knew the voice. It was Abel Hoke.

He came closer, visible now in the moonlight. He caught my eye for a moment and gave me one of those nods before he turned back to the Rebel officer. "Sure would be a shame to let one of our officers die, especially if the enemy is willing to let the doc treat him."

"That's enough, drummer," the officer said.

I could feel my colonel's eyes on me. His grip on my shoulder tightened. It felt like a threat, like he was afraid I was in league with the enemy.

Abel was as cool as the colonel. He gave me another one of those nods of his.

The Reb stepped aside and let us pass, puffing out his chest to let us know who was really in charge. "I grant you permission. Be sure to wave that white flag of yours so you don't get shot."

"Thank you." The colonel started forward. His hand was still on my shoulder. I dragged my eyes away from Abel's and went with him.

"You come back this way," the officer said.

"We've got lots of wounded on this side of the lines, too."

"I'll see you again," the colonel said. "When I come back to town."

The officer didn't know that the "doctor" was making a threat. Abel must have suspected. Still, my friend from Tennessee didn't give us away.

That was two times now that he had saved my life. He knew my father was in Washington. Why had he lied for me?

I couldn't ask. I concentrated on putting one foot in front of the other. We were in a strange kind of no-man's-land between the two armies. Each step I took should have been as familiar to me as my own home, but my town had been transformed by two armies of fighting men. With each step, I expected a bullet in my back.

How different this was from all my fancy dreams about leading men into battle, waving the Stars and Stripes as I charged the enemy. I never imagined I would be sneaking away from them, waving a white handkerchief so that my own side didn't shoot me dead. I used to be sure I would be brave in battle. Now all I wanted to do was hide.

My muscles twitched under my skin, making

me want to run, or leap into a ditch, or do anything but what I was doing. Even so, I knew that if I did run—toward the Union lines or back to Mother—one side or the other would fill me with lead.

The colonel's grip steadied me, and I was forced to keep pace with him.

The walk, just a short ways, seemed to take forever. Finally we reached the Union pickets. I raised my white handkerchief even higher and waved and waved. I waited to see a flash of fire and hear the pop of a musket. It didn't come. We were safe.

The colonel was truly a military man. The firm but respectful doctor tone he used with the Rebels was replaced with one of command. Within seconds he had identified himself and secured a messenger to get his papers to General Meade.

We went into the Wagon Hotel, where he got a quick briefing from the officer in charge. Sharpshooters had pounded holes in the roof and were shooting at the Rebel sharpshooters in Gettysburg.

I thought the colonel might leave me there, and I'd have to wave that white handkerchief all the way to the Weikert place, but he had other ideas.

"Come with me," he said. "I'll find a safe place for you before I report to General Meade."

We left the hotel and made our way to the top of Cemetery Hill. The colonel stopped and took a rifle from one dead soldier and a cartridge box from another.

"How is it that a Rebel drummer would lie to an officer for you?" the colonel asked me.

"We fed him," I said. "A few days ago when the Rebs came to town. He was starving and we fed him."

"You saved his life," the colonel said. "He returned the favor."

I didn't tell him that Abel had saved me twice, and all I had done for him was give him some food and a pair of shoes. I owed him a lot more than he owed me. But it was all too much to think on right then.

I was a jumbled mess of pride and fear and sadness. My plan had worked! I had gotten a Union colonel across enemy lines. At the same time, I knew I could have just as easily ended up dead in a heap on the ground. And I had left my mother alone, surrounded by enemy soldiers. Throughout it all I was as scared as Grace would have been.

Worse—as scared as the twins would have been.

Suddenly I was crying. I was ashamed, but I couldn't stop. I kept my head down and kept my feet moving, hoping the colonel didn't notice.

He waited for me to master my emotions.

"There are a lot of men who wouldn't have been able to take that walk with me," he said gently. "You were brave when it counted. You'd make a fine soldier."

I nodded my thanks, not trusting myself to speak.

Soon we were in the cemetery. Soldiers slept among the gravestones like living ghosts.

Colonel Braxton met with some officers in the cemetery's gatehouse. I told them everything I knew about what was happening in Gettysburg— the house-to-house searches and the barricades the Rebs had built to slow any Union advance back into town.

The officers sat on the floor around a candle stuck in a bottle, drinking coffee. They talked about what might have been if they had more troops and seemed a little bit heartened by the fact that more Union soldiers had arrived, and others were on their way.

I recognized the general—General Howard—I had taken to the top of the Fahnestock Brothers store that morning.

It was late. After midnight. I was more tired than I had ever been in my life. I went outside, sat on the ground, and looked at my town. I imagined a Sunday dinner. The whole family around the table. Father would lead the prayer. Jacob and I would tease Grace about her proper manners, and the twins would giggle while Mother scolded us to leave her be.

But we hadn't been together at the table for a long time. Tonight, enemy soldiers sat there with their Union prisoners.

The hills were alive with the sounds of Union soldiers chopping and shoveling, positioning themselves for battle. All around I heard the creaking and lumbering of artillery being pushed and pulled into place. I was relieved to see that the Union wasn't giving up after their retreat. But I was worried about Mother. What if one of those cannons was aimed at my house?

CHAPTER FIFTEEN

The Weikert Farm

I wasn't alone with my worries about Mother for long. General Howard asked me to walk with him to the top of the hill. He inspected the Union's position in the moonlight and decided that the hill and the ridge were a good place to fight.

"Will you fire on the town?" I asked.

"We'll shell the Rebels," he said. "If the citizens take to their cellars when the cannons start to roar, they'll be safe. No damage will be done to the town that can be avoided."

That didn't calm me much. I knew my mother

would be doing her best to help the wounded soldiers. I didn't believe she would go to the cellar, not when there were men who needed nursing.

"The soldiers with your mother will make sure she keeps herself safe," Colonel Braxton told me.

It was an answer meant to soothe me, not one I truly believed. I thought about trying to make my way back to town. But I knew Mother didn't want that. In the end, I decided to walk to the Weikert place like she wanted.

The colonel told General Howard he would come back shortly with General Meade, and mounted a horse.

"I need to take you somewhere safe," he said.

"My sisters are staying at a farm about a mile and a half down the Taneytown Road," I told him. "I'll go there."

"Climb on." He reached for my hand and pulled me onto the horse. "I'll take you."

I wrapped my arms around his waist. "What was in your papers?" I asked.

At first I thought he wouldn't answer. "I guess you've earned the right to know," he said finally. "We intercepted some communications between General Lee and one of his commanders. Battle plans."

"Will it help the Union win?"

The colonel shrugged. "Everything's different now. Lee planned to take Harrisburg. But now both armies have dug in here. Lee was forced to change his plans."

I asked another question. One that had been troubling me ever since I saw the waves of desperate men running through town. "Will the Union retreat again?"

I felt his back stiffen. "There will be no retreat. We'll hold this ground or die trying."

His answer was meant to reassure me, but it had the opposite effect. What if the rest of us died with them? Did the two armies ever think of that?

"What does everyone want with Gettysburg?" I asked.

"It's not Gettysburg," the colonel said. "It's an accident that we ran into each other here. But we can't let Lee win a battle on our own land. It's bad enough they've been beating us all over Virginia. If the Rebels have control of Harrisburg and Philadelphia, Washington will be totally cut off from the rest of the North.

"Lee hopes a victory in the North will give the Copperheads the political power to end the war," he continued.

The Copperheads were Northerners who wanted peace, even if it meant letting the South secede. Their opponents in Washington named them after the deadly snake because they were poison to the Union.

"We've got some Copperheads in Gettysburg," I told him. I didn't say that I was starting to wonder if they were right.

"They want peace at any cost, but I say letting the South go is too high a price," the colonel said. He steered the horse around a group of soldiers shuffling down the Taneytown Road. "Don't you worry," he told me. "Lee's not going to win this one."

Before I knew it, we were almost at the Weikert farm. I asked the colonel to let me down so I could walk the last bit. I had much to think about, and I needed to settle it in my mind before I saw Grace. I expected a good long r ound of yelling about leaving Mother alone with enemy soldiers, plus about a million questions. I wanted my mind to be clear.

"I might have need of a messenger," the colonel said. "Why don't you stay with me?"

"Me? A messenger?" I asked. For a moment I was excited. That was even better than a drummer!

"You've been brave," he told me. "You kept your head when many would have panicked."

I thought about having to run through crowds of soldiers with dispatches for the officers. The words "Got 'em" echoed in my head along with the images of all the dead men I had seen. Suddenly, being a messenger was the last thing I wanted if it meant I had to stay in the fighting.

"Thank you, sir, but I have to take care of my sisters." I was relieved to have an excuse.

The colonel nodded.

I watched him ride off, and then turned into the Weikerts' front yard. It was all torn up. I saw a light flicker in an upstairs window, and then go out. I decided to make my way to the barn rather than rouse the family. I expected to fall into a pile of hay and sleep there until morning, but that was not to be.

The screams and the moans reached me first. Then I turned the corner of the house. The barn doors were wide open. Soldiers milled around outside. Inside, the barn was crowded with wounded Union soldiers, and a few Confederates.

Men lay side by side, moaning and crying. Some pleaded for water. A few called for a doctor. Others begged to be released from life. Nurses moved among them, but there seemed to be little they could do.

On seeing me standing upright, one of them shoved a crock of beef tea and a tin cup into my hands.

"Start over there," he said, pointing to the back of the barn. "Give a swallow to anyone who can manage it."

I gripped the crock and stared. I wanted to run away screaming. Instead, I corked up my feelings and stumbled in the direction he pointed.

I knelt beside a man with blood all over his stomach. He tried to shove an envelope into my hands. "Send this to my wife," he said.

I didn't want his letter. I raised his head and tried to get him to drink, but he wouldn't.

"Take it," he moaned.

"You can send it yourself," I told him, "after the battle."

He only blinked at me. He was dying. He knew it. I knew it. I took the letter.

"Thank you," he whispered.

His eyes were already clouding over. I wanted to stay with him, but there were too many others who needed my help.

The men who were awake wanted someone to

talk to. One wanted me to pray with him, and I did. A few asked me to write letters, but I had nothing to write with, nor any paper. They all wanted to tell me where they were from—places like Wisconsin and Maine that I had never seen.

One of the Rebs was from Tennessee. He wasn't too badly wounded, but he sure wasn't looking forward to a Union prison camp.

"You know a drummer named Abel Hoke?" I asked.

The man nodded. "We're in the same company."

"I saw him a few hours ago—in Gettysburg. He's just fine," I told him.

He seemed grateful for the news. I wondered if I would see him again after the war, when I went to visit Abel.

It was still dark when I made my way back to the front of the barn to refill my crock, though it seemed as if I had been in that barn for days.

A surgeon stood in a corner covered in blood. A lantern swayed above his head. Under it, he was sawing off the arm of a soldier. The surgeon threw the limb into a wheelbarrow that was already heaped high with arms and legs and stitched the man up.

"Next!" he yelled.

Two men carried the groaning one-armed man to a spot on the floor and then brought the surgeon another soldier. His leg was mangled by a minié ball. Those bullets, favored by both the North and the South, shattered bones. There was no saving a limb if it got hit by one. I caught a whiff of chloroform, and before the soldier was even asleep, the surgeon started to saw again.

I gagged and ran out into the yard. I had to hold onto the side of the barn to stay upright. Then I gave up and sank to my knees. I knew I should go back inside, that the wounded needed help, but I could not bring myself to do it. Not right then.

CHAPTER SIXTEEN

Another Task

Thursday morning, July 2, 1863

The next thing I knew, the sun had risen. I had fallen asleep and dreamed of rumbling thunder. It was artillery fire in the distance. The battle must have resumed at first light.

It was a bright, clear day. I blinked the sleep from my eyes, feeling the sun already hot on my face. On a normal summer's day, I would be just now finishing my chores and asking Albertus McCreary if he wanted to go fishing. Instead I headed for the house, skirting a pile of arms and legs. I tried not to look at them or think about them, but the stench made me gag.

Mr. Weikert tended the outdoor oven. Mrs. Weikert, Mrs. Shriver, and others were in the kitchen, baking bread and making more beef tea. I asked after Grace.

"She's giving water to the troops out front with Tillie." Mrs. Shriver barely looked up from her bread dough. "Grab a bucket and fill it at the spring."

Sally and Jane Ann were in a corner rolling cloth into bandages under the direction of a soldier with his arm in a sling. It was a game to them. They raced the Shriver children to see who could roll the most.

I wanted to gather them in my arms, but I was afraid they would ask after Mother, and that would set them to blubbering because she wasn't here. I grabbed a bucket, filled it at the well, and saw Grace and Tillie on the edge of the road.

Grace looked fine. Tired and dirty, but fine. She smiled at the soldiers and I saw that she was almost as pretty as Tillie. I was happy to see her— a new and strange feeling for me.

I ran toward her. "Grace!"

Grace screamed and dropped her bucket.

It was only then that I looked down on myself. My shirt and trousers were covered in blood, as were my shoes.

"What happened?" Grace shrieked. "What happened?"

She was making such a racket that every soldier's eye on the Taneytown Road turned to us. She wouldn't stop shrieking long enough for me to answer.

"Calm yourself. I'm not hurt. I was helping the wounded in the barn."

Her face crumpled and she pulled me into a hug. She sobbed for a moment and then stepped back and shook herself. "Mustn't cry."

"I know," I said quietly, blinking away my own tears.

"Where's Mother?" she asked.

I picked up her bucket and put it into her hands. "She's fine," I said, hoping that was true. "I'll tell you everything. But let's give these men some water first."

Regiment after regiment passed us by on the double-quick, heading for the fighting. Too many cannons to count filled the open space to the east of us. Ammunition trains raced by. Their horses strained and sweated against the weight and the heat. One man collapsed from sunstroke and had to be carried into the house.

The soldiers were in good spirits. Thanking us.

Letting us know that they would clear Pennsylvania of the Rebs in no time.

There were some wooden boxes piled up against the fence. One soldier joked about going home in one.

"Oh, you mustn't think that way," Tillie told him.

"I'll consider myself lucky if I *get* one," the soldier joked. "I don't want to share a hole in the ground with any Rebs."

He was gone before Tillie could scold him again.

I told my story in fits and starts. Grace cringed when she heard about the Union soldiers hiding under her bed and the Rebs who found them.

"Did they touch anything?" she asked.

"Only the floor," I told her. "Soldiers don't want to have anything to do with your petticoats if that's what you're worried about."

I came to the part about finding Colonel Braxton in the carriage house, my plan, and the last Confederate officer we encountered. The one with his hand on his pistol. I might have embellished my bravery in the adventure.

"You're telling tales, William Edmonds."

Grace looked as if she had a snoot full of skunk.

I was wrong before. She wasn't pretty at all. "Am not," I said. "It's all true. Every last word of it."

"You left Mother alone in a town full of Rebs," she screeched.

"Mother has three Union soldiers guarding her along with a few wounded Rebs. She's safe no matter who's in control. And she told me to help the colonel."

With that we stopped speaking. I refilled my bucket at the spring. When I got back, some officers had just ridden up to the house. One of them was my colonel. Somehow, he had gotten his hands on another uniform. He had a saber by his side and a Colt .44 pistol at his waist.

"Will," he said, "I see you're still doing your part."

He introduced me to his fellow officers as "the boy who saved my hide."

I peeked over at Grace. She stared up at Colonel Braxton openmouthed.

"This is my sister Grace," I told him. "She specializes in catching flies."

Grace closed her mouth and squawked something or other.

The colonel tipped his hat. "Pleased to meet

you. I hope you know what a fine service your brother has done for the Union."

Then the colonel asked me to show them to the farmhouse's roof so they could see the battlefield.

I led them through the house and found the trapdoor leading up to the roof. The officers used field glasses to survey the landscape. Then the colonel let me look through them, too. Dust and smoke filled the air, and there seemed to be soldiers everywhere my eye landed. Cannons were being rushed into position. Infantry soldiers were forming lines. Officers galloped back and forth.

From this distance, it was easy to put aside thoughts of the bloody men in the barn, and the pile of limbs that no one had had time to bury. War was a glorious adventure again, if only for a moment. I slipped into one of my old daydreams. I saw myself galloping across the battlefield, waving the flag to inspire the men. They cheered my bravery as I raced by.

I lowered the field glasses with a sigh. Had Jacob had the same kind of dreams that I did? I wondered how he had felt when real bullets and shells began to fly.

The colonel asked me to name the landmarks. The hills—Big Round Top and Little Round

Top—were just to our west. The Lutheran Seminary on the other side of town was now in Confederate hands.

"I watched the battle begin from there," I told them. Then I pointed east. "That's Culp's Hill, and you see Cemetery Hill where we were last night."

Colonel Braxton checked what I told him against a map. He and the others tried to figure the number of Rebs and noted their positions. Then he rolled up the map and handed it to me.

"Now that you know your sister is safe, I have another task for you," he said.

★ CHAPTER SEVENTEEN ★

The Snapping Turtle

The colonel pointed to the Leister farmhouse, just a little way up the Taneytown Road, where men in blue milled about. "General Meade has set up his headquarters there," he said. "Take this to him. Tell him it's from Colonel Braxton."

I didn't see any shelling in that direction, so I said I would.

We made our way down into the front yard again, and I watched the colonel mount his horse. "I know I can count on you," he said. "Give it directly to General Meade, no one else. No telling how long before he'll see it otherwise."

He and the officers set off across the fields, galloping toward the battle.

I headed straight for General Meade, not stopping to tell Grace. I didn't want to set her to squawking again. I had to push my way into the river of blue that was marching by. It took me some minutes to work my way through them, and then I set off running alongside the road.

"What's your hurry?" some of the soldiers teased.

"The Rebs will still be there," another said. "No need to run."

I paid them no mind. I got to the house in no time and asked for General Meade. An aide tried to take the map from me.

"Colonel Braxton told me to put it into his hands myself," I said. "And no one else."

The aide didn't like it, but he led me into the parlor where General Meade was studying some papers. The aide cleared his throat.

"Yes, what is it?" the general asked.

I could see why the men called him the Snapping Turtle. His head was small for his body and he was kind of google-eyed.

"This boy has something for you, from Colonel Braxton."

The general held out his hand and I passed him the map. "Colonel Braxton said to give it to you and no one else," I said.

The men around him peered over his shoulder and talked about where to send what regiments. I watched them and wondered what I should do. I had never been near a man of such importance before. Should I stay in case he had another task for me? Should I go?

The aide cleared his throat again. The general blinked at us, looking more and more like a turtle.

"I live in town," I told him. "If you have any questions about the map."

He seemed to see me for the first time then. He took in the blood on my shirt. "Are you hurt?"

"No, sir," I stammered. "I was helping the wounded up at the Weikert farm. The Jacob Weikert farm—there are at least two other Weikert farms." I was babbling, but somehow I couldn't stop. "Lots of Weikerts around Gettysburg. I'm the only Edmonds that I know of."

The men around Meade chuckled, but the general eyed me seriously.

"Thank you for your service," he said. "The wounded need you more than we do."

I nodded and backed out of the room.

The next thing I knew I was racing along the road again. There were fewer troops marching by. Grace and Tillie were in the house, and I joined them. They were too busy to notice that I had even been gone. The gunfire was constant now, and we did our best to stay away from the windows. I peeked once and saw dead bodies in the grass. It was too dangerous to try to move them out of the sun.

The constant roar of cannons and rifles forced us to shout, and we all grew hoarse as the afternoon went on. The farmhouse shook. Our throats ached. The twins hid in a closet with their hands over their ears.

In the middle of the afternoon, there was a sudden quiet. We stared at each other, stunned. I wondered if the battle was over and who had won. But the quiet only lasted for a minute or two. Then, suddenly, the cannons on the Round Tops began to roar. I shouted to Grace to take cover, but I couldn't even hear my own voice.

Soldiers scrambled. Shells flew overhead. The whole house shook.

In a lull, a soldier suggested we move to a farmhouse about a half-mile across the fields to the east. Mrs. Shriver and her mother, Mrs. Weikert, were determined to go, and so we set off. Grace had Jane Ann on her back, and I carried Sally on mine.

We raced across the field, hearing explosions behind us and above us. A shell fell just a half a field away, sending dirt flying. We had only been at the farmhouse for a few minutes when another soldier sent us back where we had come from.

"You're in more danger here!" he yelled. "Those shells from the Round Tops will fly right over your house and land here!"

As if to prove his point, a shell exploded in front of the house, sending dirt and rocks flying into the air. The earth trembled beneath our feet.

Grace and I pulled the twins onto our backs again while Mrs. Weikert and Mrs. Shriver took charge of her two young ones. I could not tell what the little ones were thinking. The twins suddenly seemed younger than they did two days ago. Sally had taken to sucking her thumb again, a habit Mother broke her of last year, and Jane Ann hadn't spoken a word since we started out. Nor did she cry.

On our way back across the field I tried to see Gettysburg. There was a big cloud of smoke above it, and I couldn't make out any of the buildings. Was the town on fire? Had it been shelled until there was nothing left? Grace and I eyed each other. No doubt we shared the same worry. Had Mother been hurt?

There was no way to find out. The women went right back to the kitchen when we returned to the Weikert place. We hadn't even been gone long enough for the bread in the oven to burn. I settled Sally and Jane Ann in a back room, along with the Shriver children. Then I stole to the roof, determined to get a look at Gettysburg.

I couldn't see it. It was too far away and Cemetery Hill blocked my view. I couldn't see anything clearly without field glasses, but there was terrible fighting going on in Sherby's peach orchard, and what used to be a wheat field was covered with bodies and blood. I closed my eyes and said a prayer for Mother, and then one for Jacob and one for Father. Then I got back to work caring for the wounded.

A couple of hours later I heard some soldiers talking.

"The Rebels are on this side of the Round Tops, coming toward the house."

"If they hit the Taneytown Road, we're lost."

Mr. Weikert and I went to the south side of the house and looked to the hills. Rebels were indeed moving toward us—fast.

Even as my mind raced with possibilities, my feet were rooted on the spot. I had to make sure Grace and the twins were in a safe place. There was no way down to the cellar from inside the house. What was more dangerous—staying in the house or making a run for the cellar doors? Should I take a rifle from one of the dead and try to hold the Rebels back? I wasn't even sure I could get the dang thing loaded and ready to fire before they were in the yard.

Then suddenly I heard the sound of a fife and drum coming from the other side of the barn.

"Here come the Pennsylvania Reserves!" Mr. Weikert yelled.

They marched at the double-quick, firing as they ran.

The Rebels fired back.

The Pennsylvania men kept going, ignoring the bullets.

The Rebels stopped, turned, and began to retreat.

I was still rooted in my spot. A few minutes ago I thought we were lost, and now the Rebels were retreating. Mr. Weikert cheered. I tried to join him, but my eyes fell on two dead bodies and the sound got stuck in my throat.

Had either side gained anything in that brief skirmish?

That night, the number of wounded that were brought to the farm was terrible. Litter bearers carried the worst of them. Others limped in on their own two feet, often carrying comrades on their backs. The barn was so crowded it could hold no more. There were men all over the house. Finally we had to lay them outside in the orchard and around the buildings.

Grace and I were too busy to do more than nod at each other occasionally. The soldiers who weren't injured too badly did what they could to help, including a New Hampshire man with a leg wound who sat and minded the children. Every time I looked in on the twins, they were in the middle of a game or a story or a song. How he managed to keep their minds off the battle I'll never know.

The rest of us did whatever we could to help the wounded. But there were too many of them and too few of us. The number of dead grew. A couple of soldiers dug a pit and rolled at least ten bodies into it before they threw dirt on top again. It was truly a horrible thing to behold.

When I could not stand up anymore, I found a patch of ground and went to sleep, hoping for something better tomorrow.

My wish didn't come true. I woke to fierce cannonading early Friday morning, coming from the direction of Culp's Hill. The windows rattled and the crockery trembled on the shelves. Still, the women kept baking bread, and I kept carrying bread and beef tea to the wounded. There was nothing else we could do. Until, on one of my trips back to the kitchen, I noticed soldiers setting up cannons right outside the house.

We were about to find ourselves on the battle's front lines.

A Reb Prisoner

Friday morning, July 3, 1863

T he soldiers sent us to the cellar. Jane Ann
clung to me, tight around my neck. Grace
carried Sally. We crept out of the kitchen and
stayed close to the house, skirting around the side
single file until we came to the cellar doors. Mr.
Weikert threw them open and the women started
down the stairs.

The yard was still full of wounded and a group
of Rebel prisoners. They had no cellar to hide
in and there was no room for them to join us. I
wondered what would happen to those left out in
the open. A shell screamed overhead. Another hit

not too far away, sending dirt and smoke into the air. Artillerymen raced past me to fire the Union cannons.

I was at the cellar doors handing Jane Ann to Grace when I saw him.

A little Reb prisoner, smaller than me, stumbled toward the well. He was covered in dirt and blood. A drum, or what was left of it, hung about his neck, and his arm was cocked in an odd way. A Union guard said something, and he gave a funny little nod.

Abel!

"I'll be back," I screamed to Grace.

She tried to argue with me, but Mr. Weikert scrambled into the cellar and closed the doors behind them.

I got to Abel just as he crumpled. He groaned when I touched him and I tried not to jostle his arm when I laid him on the ground. The sun beat down fiercely, and heat seemed to be coming off his body in waves. A shell must have exploded right in front of him. He was covered in dirt. I couldn't tell where the blood was coming from, but his face was covered.

"Abel," I said. "Abel it's me."

He didn't answer. He didn't even nod.

Some men, most of them Rebel prisoners, were trying to get water from the well. There was no way to bring up the water bucket.

"Where's the crank?" a Union officer asked me.

I nodded in the direction of the cellar. The spring had run completely dry. When Mr. Weikert saw that the soldiers were taking water from his well, he had removed the crank.

"I've already lost all of my crops and most of my livestock," he had said when he saw me watching. "I won't have them pump my well dry, too. My farm won't survive without water."

My heart lurched when I saw how desperate the men were for water—especially Abel.

The Union officer marched off. He came back with his pistol in one hand and the crank in the other. Someone brought up the water bucket and I filled Abel's canteen.

I forced some water between his lips. Most of it ran to the ground, but some went down his throat. I used the rest to clean the dirt and blood out of his nose, ears, and eyes. Blood poured down his face and I saw a gash on his forehead, just over one eye.

Then I saw that his left hand was smashed and bleeding. I poured water over it and he screamed louder than the shells. His face was twisted in pain and he tried to roll away from me.

I grabbed his shoulders and tried to hold him down. He was half-crazed with pain. I screamed right in his ear to be heard over the roar of the shells. "Abel! Abel Hoke!" I yelled. "It's me, Will Edmonds. From Gettysburg."

His eyelids fluttered, and he groaned.

"I'm going to get help," I said. "I'll be back."

His head gave one of those funny little nods, and I knew he would hang on to life for the next little while at least.

I ran for one of the surgeons in the barn.

"I have a hundred men in front of him," the surgeon told me. His apron was soaked through with blood. Bits of blood and skin hung from the saw in his hand as one man was lifted off the table and another placed in front of him. The injured man screamed while the doctor poked around in his wound, then the chloroform took hold. The doctor raised his saw and I stumbled away.

The noise was dreadful. Men moaned, shells screamed, bullets popped. Every once in a while

I could hear one of those eerie Rebel yells above the rest of the ruckus. Each time, it sent a shiver up my spine.

I tried another surgeon and got the same answer.

I was suddenly overwhelmed with sadness. Abel had already lost his father. Was he going to die without seeing his mama again, or his sisters and brothers? I felt helpless.

"He's just a boy," I choked. Tears were streaming down my cheeks. "A drummer boy."

"Carry him in," the surgeon said, pointing to an area that was filled with wounded men waiting for treatment. "I'll get to him when I can."

I trudged back to Abel and tried to rouse him again. I poured more water down his throat and it only made him gag. He rolled onto his side and started spitting out dirt and water.

A Rebel officer limped over. He pointed to the gash in Abel's forehead. "That'll heal," he said. He poked at Abel's arm.

Abel's face twisted in pain again, but he didn't seem to have the energy to scream.

"That hand is gonna have to come off," the Rebel said calmly. "If he lives long enough to see a surgeon."

That wasn't what I wanted to hear, and I didn't want him giving Abel any ideas about dying. I pushed the officer away.

"He's crazy," I said to Abel. "You're not gonna die. You hear me?"

Abel groaned again. I could take him to the cellar. Grace would help me nurse him. He would be out of the heat, but was that enough to save his life? There was too much blood. He needed a doctor—now.

Then it hit me. Colonel Braxton. Abel had saved Colonel Braxton's life. The colonel would make sure Abel got the help he needed. But first I had to get Abel to Meade's headquarters.

"Abel," I said, yelling into his ear. "I'm taking you to the colonel, the one whose life you saved."

He groaned, and his eyelids fluttered again. He licked his lips. "Wawtah," he said quietly.

I filled the canteen again and poured some water into his mouth. This time he swallowed and took some more. Then I dumped the rest over his head. The cool water revived him some.

I sat him up against the side of the barn and crouched with my back in front of him.

"Put your good arm around my neck," I commanded.

He moaned. His head lolled to one side.

"Abel," I shouted. "You have to try. I have to take you to the colonel for help."

He nodded. I guess he understood.

I turned my back to him again. "Put your arm around my neck."

That time he did. I slipped my hands under his knees and held them in the crook of my arms. I got to my feet slowly, afraid that he would let go and flop over backward. He didn't. He hung on with his one good arm, and let the other dangle at my side. He was nothing but skin and bones, barely heavier than Jane Ann.

I wished I could stop and tell Grace what I was doing. I wanted to get a look at my sisters, to fix their faces in my mind in case—

"You'll see them later," I told myself. Saying it out loud made me feel a little better.

The fighting on Culp's Hill had stopped. To whose advantage I didn't know. I trudged ahead, concentrating on putting one foot in front of the other, skirting the bloated body of a dead horse and stepping over dead men, their bodies burned black by the sun. Just two days ago I had to look away from the eyes of a dead man. Now I barely noticed them as anything more than another hurdle in my path. I couldn't stop to think about the fact that each one of them had been alive the day before. That each one of them had a family like me, like Abel.

Abel's body grew heavier with each step. He was quiet for much too long. Was I carrying a dead man? I jostled him, and he moaned.

Sweat poured down my face. His blood was hot and sticky on my shirt. Finally, I collapsed along the side of the road. There was no shade. No relief from the sun. I grabbed a cap from a dead Union man and used it to fan my friend. Blood still poured freely from his arm.

I rested for a few moments and then got to my feet again. Abel was breathing, but I could not rouse him to put his arms around my neck again. He didn't even wince when I touched him, but I could see he was still breathing. I grabbed him by the waist and tried to throw him over my shoulder. My arms and legs shook with exhaustion.

Men were waiting in the hot stillness. One offered to help me with Abel, but I worried what would happen when they realized he was a Reb. Finally I had to admit that I could not carry him alone.

A Wisconsin man carried him for me.

"You a Reb?" he asked me.

I shook my head. "I live in Gettysburg."

His face was streaked with dirt and sweat. His eyes were tired and sad, but they were gentle when they looked at Abel.

"He's just a boy," I said.

The man nodded and kept walking.

My eyes were focused on a tree just outside Meade's headquarters. Shade—blessed shade. I asked him to set Abel down there, and he leaned him up against the tree.

I gave Abel some water from the canteen, and once again it dribbled out of his mouth. I poured a little over his head, and then he was able to swallow some. "I'll be back," I told him. "I'll be right back with the colonel."

There was no response.

"Do you hear me, Abel Hoke?" I yelled. "Do you want to go home to that mama of yours in Tennessee?"

His eyelids fluttered, and then he gave me one of those funny little nods.

Soldiers milled about outside waiting for orders. Some read their Bibles. A few wrote letters home. I witnessed some men writing their names on their arms, so they could be identified if they were killed. Most simply stared into space.

I ran into Meade's headquarters, pushing past the guards who tried to block my way. "Colonel Braxton!" I yelled. "Colonel Braxton!"

"Braxton isn't here," an officer told me. "What's this about?"

"I need a surgeon."

"Is Braxton hurt?" the officer asked.

Would they send a surgeon to Colonel Braxton? One who wouldn't be spared for a Rebel drummer? I looked right into the officer's eyes. "He needs a surgeon."

"Wait here." The officer marched off and came back a few minutes later with a surgeon. He carried a medical kit.

"Take this man to Colonel Braxton," the officer told me.

I nodded and led the way.

The surgeon startled when he saw Abel.

"I lied, but this drummer saved Colonel Braxton's life and I know the colonel would want to return the favor. I couldn't get the other surgeons to look at him."

He knelt beside Abel and examined his forehead. "Just a scratch." He stood and started to walk away.

"His arm," I yelled. "His hand."

The surgeon came back.

Abel yelled something fierce when the surgeon checked his arm. He pushed and pulled Abel's shoulder and it seemed to go right back to where it belonged in Abel's body rather than hanging at that funny angle.

His hand wasn't so easy to fix. The surgeon lifted Abel in his arms and started toward the house. "It has to come off," he said. "The bones are smashed."

I ran behind him. He carried Abel into what used to be a dining room. A long board was propped up on the backs to two chairs. There was blood all over and the air was thick with chloroform. A couple of injured men sat against the wall while medical people moved about. Flies buzzed around the open window. There was a pile of limbs just outside.

The doctor set Abel down on one of the boards and grabbed a knife. I closed my eyes and by the time I opened them it was all over. Abel's hand was gone and the stump was bandaged.

"Get some food and water into him if you can,"

the surgeon said. "I've done all I can. Let's hope he doesn't get a surgical fever. It's in God's hands now."

A couple of soldiers came by with a litter and carried Abel back outside. I asked them to let him down under the same tree.

I watched Abel's chest moving up and down. Was it my imagination or were his breaths smaller than they had been before?

Colonel Braxton walked over a few minutes later. "I hear I've been gravely injured," he said.

"This is the Reb drummer who saved your life," I told him. "It was the only way I could get help." My voice caught. I had to fight to keep the tears back. "He's not a drummer anymore—not without a hand."

Colonel Braxton peered into my face. "Are you the boy from Gettysburg?"

I nodded, looking down at myself so that he wouldn't see my tears. It was only then that I noticed that my clothes were covered in blood and dirt. I imagine my face was covered, too. I hadn't changed my clothes in three days.

"It's me," I said. "Will Edmonds. I've been at the farm, helping the wounded. Then I found Abel."

The colonel crouched in front of Abel. "What did the surgeon say?"

"He'll live or he'll die." My voice caught again. "I don't know what happened to him," I blurted. "There's too many dead."

"Yes," he said with a solemn expression. "Too many."

I wondered how many friends he had lost since the war began.

The colonel patted my arm. "I'll try to find a wagon to bring him to a hospital. We won't let your friend die if we can help it."

Suddenly the quiet was broken by a sharp report from enemy lines, followed by another. There was a pause of a few seconds and then the sky opened up. Only it wasn't thunder and rain. It was artillery shells.

★ CHAPTER NINETEEN ★

"This'll decide it!"

Friday afternoon, July 3, 1863

T his wasn't like the shelling of the past few
days. This was ten times louder. Men fell to
their knees just from the sound of it.

"This'll decide it!" Colonel Braxton yelled. He
seemed excited. "This battle will end here." He
ran toward the headquarters, shouting something
over his shoulder.

I couldn't hear him. The Confederate guns
roared and ours answered. The ground that trembled before now shook. My teeth rattled in my
mouth, and I could barely stand. A shell hit
Meade's headquarters, sending men dashing out-

side. Others hit the fields around me, making deep gouges, like graves, in the earth. One minute a man was standing there, and the next he was just a bunch of parts, scattering in ten different directions.

Water was all I had in my stomach, but I heaved it up all the same. Smoke was all around me. There was so much saltpeter in the air, the taste of it filled my mouth.

I focused my eyes on Abel so that I wouldn't see any more flying body parts. There was nowhere to go. I had dragged him right into the thick of the battle. I crouched over him while shells flew overhead, convinced I was going to get the both of us killed. Thank goodness I hadn't brought Grace and the twins with me.

"They're safe in the cellar," I whispered. "Safe in the cellar."

Abel groaned, whether from pain or the noise I couldn't tell.

"Don't you die on me," I screamed. "You saved my life and I aim to return the favor. Don't you die on me!"

Just as suddenly as the shelling started, it stopped. I had seen enough over the past three days to know what that meant. When the shelling stopped, the infantry took over. Cannons were replaced with rifles, artillery shells with bullets and bayonets.

I put my hand on Abel's chest and felt it rise and fall, rise and fall. He was still breathing.

Through the smoke, infantry soldiers moved ghostlike into position. When the smoke finally cleared, most of them were gone. My ears were ringing, but at the same time the quiet was spooky after all that noise.

A soldier ran out of what was left of Meade's headquarters. "Get yourself away from here," he yelled.

I looked at my friend. He couldn't walk, and I was too done in to carry him. Besides, was there any place safe?

"Go," Abel groaned. "Go."

"I'm not leaving you," I said.

Abel gave me one of those funny nods—he would not have left me either—and then he seemed to pass out again.

All around us was confusion. The air was heavy with gunpowder. Knapsacks, blankets, and guns were strewn everywhere. A few officers stood in front of headquarters, tension written all over their faces. I spotted a pair of field glasses a short distance away and ran for them.

I climbed the tree above us, anxious to know what was happening and to look for a safer place to bring Abel. The Rebel infantry marched out from the cover of trees on Seminary Ridge by McMillan's orchard. The Union men were scrambling into position on Cemetery Ridge. A broad field sat between them.

Two long lines of Rebels marched into that field and started to cross it. The lines must have been a mile wide. It was hard to believe that there were that many soldiers still standing after all the wounded I had seen.

They were silent. No Rebel yell. No double-quick. It was a grim, steady march. They crossed the Emmitsburg Road and kept coming.

Why were our men not shooting?

When the Rebs were close—too close—our big guns opened up again. Rebs fell in waves. They didn't retreat. They didn't run. They simply closed ranks and kept coming.

Soon our cannon fire was replaced with musket fire. Beyond the smoke toward Seminary Ridge I expected to see Rebels running away, back to their own lines. There were none. Had they broken the Union lines? Had they pushed past the infantry?

Suddenly, it was quiet. The bullets stopped and were replaced by cheers. But who was cheering? Who had won?

Once again, the smoke cleared. The field was full of dead, gray-clad men. The boys in blue were cheering. There was no retreat. The Rebels had kept coming until every last one of them was dead or taken prisoner.

I guessed the Union had won, but what did they win? What did all that killing amount to?

Tears streamed down my face. I climbed down to join Abel. He was asleep, but I spoke to him anyway. I had to say the words out loud, if only to convince myself. "It's over," I told him. "I think we're safe for now."

No one seemed to know what would happen next. I heard more fighting from the direction of the Weikert farm and I called out to a soldier coming from that direction.

"Is there fighting there?" I asked.

"There's fighting everywhere," he answered.

I remembered Mother's words to me in the kitchen before I left. "Find the girls at the Weikert farm and wait out the battle there. It will be safer," and the scared, angry look on Grace's face when I didn't go down into the cellar.

There was nothing I could do. No way right then to know for sure they were alive and well. I focused on Abel. About the time the sun was setting, his eyes flickered. The air had cooled a bit, but his skin was so hot it was like touching fire. He tried to sit up and raved like a madman, insisting that he had to find his drum, join his company.

"My daddy's waiting," he kept saying. "My daddy's waiting."

I didn't have the heart to tell him that his daddy was dead. I was even afraid to go and find the surgeon in case Abel found the energy to get up and leave.

"No," I said. "Your daddy said to wait right here."

I poured water over his head, hoping that would cool him down some. Then I grabbed a cap and fanned him like crazy.

After a few minutes he fell asleep again. Was this the fever the doctor spoke of? Would it kill him?

"Dang it! I didn't carry you all the way here

and lie to a general's aide for you to go and die on me."

Men were moving around us, collecting the dead and the wounded. A Union man came near but I wouldn't let him take Abel. They wouldn't take care of him like I would. I didn't want him to end up dead, or a prisoner.

Abel woke up a few hours later and started raving again. I poured more water over his head. I had managed to find some bread and some beef tea. I gave him as much as he would take. I couldn't remember the last time I had eaten.

One soldier nearby was munching on a piece of hardtack. Jacob had written to us about how awful hardtack tasted. About how the biscuits were hard enough to break a tooth. About how they were full of weevils. But I hadn't eaten in a very long time. The soldier saw me eyeing it and I guess I looked as hungry as I felt. He threw me a biscuit.

I gnawed off a bite and held it in my mouth for a long time before it was soft enough to chew. On a normal day I might turn my nose up at such a thing, but today it was the sweetest thing I had ever eaten.

My colonel never came back. I wondered if he

was dead, but I was too tired to worry about him much. With the hardtack in my belly, I lay down next to Abel. I kept my hand on his chest so I could feel it rise and fall, and drifted off to sleep.

CHAPTER TWENTY

By the Dawn's Early Light

Saturday morning, July 4, 1863

I t was near dawn when I heard movement around me. I sat up, rubbing my eyes. The soldiers slapped each other on their backs. I heard cheers coming from inside Meade's headquarters.

"What happened?" I asked.

"The Rebels are withdrawing from the town," a soldier told me. "We're fixing to march into Gettysburg."

My heart leaped. The Rebels were withdrawing. My family was safe. Soon we would all be together again. I wanted to race into town and find Mother.

Abel must have heard, and it was like he could

read my thoughts. "Where's your mama?" he asked.

"In town," I said. "You were injured. I brought you here." I touched his face. He wasn't nearly as hot as he was last night.

He pushed himself up on his elbows. "Got to get to your mama's house," he mumbled.

His face was still pale, but not the same deadly white it had been yesterday afternoon. "You're not strong enough," I told him. "And I can't carry you that far."

"Your mama," he said, stronger this time. "She'll be worried."

He dragged himself to a seated position. He looked at his bandaged hand and then at me.

"It's gone," I told him.

I thought that would take everything out of him, but he only nodded. Then he grasped the tree trunk with his good hand and pulled himself up. He wobbled for a second before letting go. He was as unsteady as a new colt, but he was on his own feet.

"Let's go see your mama."

"Are you crazy?" I asked. "You almost died. You've got a surgical fever. You can't march into Gettysburg."

"You go then," he said.

"I'm not leaving you alone here."

"Then take me with you," Abel insisted.

Finally I agreed. "We have to take it slow." I pulled his good arm over my shoulder and wrapped mine around his waist. He said he didn't want my help, but he was as useless as a shot-up drum.

We fell in line behind a column of soldiers and slowly made our way forward. The military band at the front played familiar patriotic songs like "Battle Cry of Freedom" and "The Star-Spangled Banner," but everything else seemed unreal and unfamiliar.

Taneytown Road was so torn up by wagons and shells that we stuck to the fields, eventually making it to the Evergreen Cemetery. It was a strange and blighted place in the early morning light. I hardly would have recognized it as the site of Sunday strolls.

Grave markers were overturned and broken. The grass was trampled into mud, flower beds were black with gunpowder, and body after body lay above the ground instead of below it. At first I thought the dead had been unearthed, but these were soldiers. The new dead, not the old.

Rain started to fall, like heaven itself was weeping.

The carnage got worse as we headed toward town. Battle debris was all around us. Broken down artillery wagons, guns, knapsacks, cartridge boxes, coats, and shoes were strewn about, along with letters, photographs, and even Bibles. There was a long line of unburied men, so black and bloated that I could not tell which side they fought for, nor did I care.

I strained to get a look at my house, but it was too dark and too far away still. My eyes darted here and there, looking for some assurance of the civilians' safety, but there was none.

As the sky lightened, I could see that houses were peppered with bullet holes. The Rupp house had no windows left at all, and there were two dead men on the porch. One Rebel sharpshooter was slumped over dead, half in and half out of a garret window farther down Baltimore Street.

The smell was overpowering. Worse than when we found the dead rat under the floorboards at school. Worse than a thousand overflowing privies. I tried to breathe through my mouth so that the stench would not overwhelm me, but then it filled my mouth and made me gag.

The sun was beginning to rise. Folks peered out their windows and opened their doors. They seemed dazed at first, then waved handkerchiefs. Their voices joined with the band.

> *Oh, say can you see by the dawn's early light*
> *What so proudly we hailed at the twilight's*
> *last gleaming?*
> *Whose broad stripes and bright stars through*
> *the perilous fight,*
> *O'er the ramparts we watched were so gallantly*
> *streaming?*
> *And the rocket's red glare, the bombs bursting*
> *in air,*
> *Gave proof through the night that our flag*
> *was still there.*
> *Oh, say does that Star-Spangled Banner*
> *yet wave*
> *O'er the land of the free and the home of*
> *the brave?*

I could see the flag now at the front of our long column. How many times had I imagined myself marching behind it, celebrating a glorious Union victory? How many times had I imagined myself a hero?

I never imagined the destruction, or the stench. I never imagined the dead.

There was muted talk from the townspeople as we marched by. Someone remembered that it was Independence Day. We hurrahed for the Fourth of July and in gratitude to the soldiers. One comment stood out above all the rest, though.

"Jennie Wade was killed," someone said. "In her sister's kitchen. Baking bread for the Union soldiers."

I stopped short with a gasp. Abel stumbled beside me. "Were any other townspeople hurt?"

She didn't know. No one knew.

I strained to get a look at my house. Would there be bullet holes? Had Mother been killed in her kitchen, too? I wanted to break into a run. Abel could tell. My steps had quickened and he couldn't keep up with me.

"Run," he said. "Run to your mama. Make sure . . ."

It was like someone had drummed the order to charge on my heart. But I forced myself to slow down. "No." I took a shaky breath. "We'll go together."

We skirted a Rebel barricade made of fences and bedposts and other pieces of furniture, and finally we were at my door. Grace's red shawl still hung from the upstairs window.

Grace! How would I tell Grace and the twins if—

The front door was locked. I pounded on it, holding my breath. I thought my heart might jump right out of my body.

A man—a Rebel—opened the door. "More wounded," he said over his shoulder. Then to me. "Take him to the Courthouse, or the church on the corner. We're full up."

I nearly dropped Abel. The Rebel caught him and sat him on the pavement, against the house.

"I live here! This is my house." I pushed past the man and looked for Mother.

The parlor was filled with wounded. A Union man moved among them on a crutch made from a fence post. He held a basket of biscuits. Mother must be in the kitchen, baking biscuits, I thought. I jumped over the men and went to find her there, but I only saw two soldiers taking more biscuits out of the oven. I fell against the back door. There were two dead men in the yard, but I still could not see my mother. Where was she? I thought of Jennie Wade and I wanted to scream.

I ran back into the parlor and was about to run upstairs when someone grabbed my arm. I tried to twist out of his grasp, but he was too strong for me.

"Where is my mother?" I demanded. "What have you done with her?"

★ CHAPTER TWENTY-ONE ★

"Where is my mother?"

W hy was no one answering?

"Where is my mother?" I asked again. It came out a whisper. I was suddenly full of tears. My throat closed up around them.

I recognized the Union man we had taken in that first day, the one who had argued with his Rebel guards over dinner. His answer seemed to take ten years.

"She's at the Courthouse," he said. "We made biscuits and she took some over. She's been worried about you."

I slumped against the wall and took deep breaths to try and calm myself.

"Where've you been?" the soldier asked. "We thought you were on a farm."

"I was," I choked out. "But the battle . . ." I couldn't finish.

"Your sisters?" he asked.

"Safe, I think. I had to leave," I said, remembering Abel. "My friend is out front. He needs a clean bandage and a place to rest."

We stepped aside while two men I didn't recognize—one with a bandage on his arm, the other with a limp—carried a body down the stairs.

"Looks like a bed just opened up," the Union man told me.

I met Mother on my way to the Courthouse. She was coming back with an empty basket. She walked right past me.

"Mother!" I said.

She turned to look at me.

"Mother," I said again.

She peered at me.

"It's me. Will," I said. I caught a glimpse of myself in the Pierce's parlor window. My face was covered in blood and dirt. My shirt was as stiff as Abel's bandage, and my trousers and shoes were crusted with mud.

I took off my cap and showed her the tuft of hair that was forever sticking up. The one Grace was always tugging me by. "See, it's me."

Mother dropped her basket and screamed.

"I'm not hurt. Just dirty."

She pulled me toward her, dirt and all. We stood there hugging for the longest time, and I wasn't even mortified by my public tears.

"Are the girls with you?" Mother asked when she finally pulled away. "We heard there was heavy fighting at the Round Tops. I can't believe I sent my babies away to be safe, and you wound up right in the middle of the worst of it."

"I left them at the farm yesterday afternoon," I said. "They were safe in the cellar."

Mother closed her eyes and sighed.

"I brought Abel home with me," I said. "I found him wounded. That's why I had to leave. I had to get help for him."

I picked up Mother's basket, took her hand, and led her toward our house.

"Any chance I'll be able to take a bath?" I asked.

Mother stopped and stared at me for the longest time. "Are you sure you're William Edmonds?" she asked. Then she threw her head back and laughed until she cried.

I guess I never volunteered to take a bath before.

There were violent thunderstorms that night. General Lee used the cover of rain and darkness to begin his long retreat south. Some said the line of ambulances and wagons stretched for seventeen miles. We were finally free of Confederate soldiers—those who could walk, anyway.

The battle might have been over, but our problems weren't. Abel's fever came and went. He slept most of the time. Sometimes he woke up ranting and raving. Other times he was almost himself. We kept bathing him with cool water and changing his bandage, but for a few days I was sure he was going to die.

We had almost nothing to feed him to build up his strength. All our food stores were gone. Every house in town was in the same predicament. A quart of beans had to suffice for the people in our home that day, and others in town had nothing at all. The army's supply wagons hadn't kept up with the soldiers. Most of the farmer's fields for miles and miles around were destroyed, and the nearest working railroad station was twenty miles away.

Somehow, the world learned of our predicament. The first wagon filled with food rolled into town on Sunday evening. By Monday, both the Christian and the Sanitary Commissions brought wagons full of food and medical supplies. I watched them ride down Baltimore Street from our doorway. A man handed me an orange. I was so hungry that I ate the whole thing, skin and all. Then I begged another for Abel.

I peeled it for him, and he ate it slowly, wedge by wedge. A drop of juice stood on his lip and he licked it up before it could dry.

"That's the best orange I've ever had," he said.

I agreed. It was sweeter than anything in Petey Winter's candy store.

I wished I could hold the orange smell of it in my nose forever to cover up the stench all around. The Union army had left behind soldiers to bury the dead, but the task was enormous, and slow. Some said you could smell Gettysburg as far away as Harrisburg.

Mother had bottles of peppermint and pennyroyal oil in the kitchen. "Put this under your nose," she said, handing one to me. "It'll block the smell."

Abel and I tried each one. He thought the pennyroyal worked best, but I favored the peppermint.

Even in the terrible heat, we kept our windows closed. The sky was full of flies, buzzards, and crows.

Aunt Bess surprised us on Monday. She came to the door, rolled up her sleeves, and commenced to scrubbing blood off the walls. "My house is gone," she said. "But I'm alive and I'm *free*."

Many people came to our door that day. Another invasion of sorts began almost as soon as the soldiers left. People arrived hunting for their wounded or their dead. Newspapermen were on their heels.

I had no stomach for telling stories. I stayed with Abel and helped Mother as much as I could with the wounded and the cleanup.

A soldier had come by on Sunday with the word that Grace and the twins were safe. Mother and I decided that they were best off in the country, at least until the injured men could be moved out of

our house and to one of the churches. We asked
a soldier who was heading out to the Round Tops
to stop at the Weikert place and let her know that
I would come to get them as soon as I could.

Grace, being Grace, didn't listen.

★ CHAPTER TWENTY-TWO ★

Reunions

Tuesday, July 7, 1863

I was coming back from the church when I saw
them. A scraggly group on the top of the Baltimore Street hill. More gawkers, I thought. More
mouths to fill. Then I saw the four little ones. It
was Grace and the twins with Mrs. Shriver, Tillie
Pierce, and the Shriver children.

I was relieved to see them all walking upright.
No one appeared injured. No telling what they
had seen on their way here. The bodies in town
had been buried by Union soldiers—their own
men first, and then the Confederates. I didn't
know about those in the fields outside of town.

Some were in graves so shallow that feet stuck out of the earth. Countless dead animals had yet to be burned.

I had spent a day picking up debris the soldiers had left behind. Abel was still in bed, but he helped me go through the letters and diaries, looking for clues as to whom they belonged to, so as to send them on to their loved ones.

"This one is cut off right in the middle of a sentence," he had said, turning the paper over.

I'd stared at a picture of a little girl—younger than the twins—in a leather case, hoping that her father had only dropped the picture and was not among the dead.

Now I shook off my sadness and prepared to meet my sisters.

Grace spied me, let out a screech, and started to run.

Uh-oh, I thought. Was she still mad at me for not going into the cellar on the day I had found Abel?

When she was within hearing distance I tried to tell her I couldn't help it, but Grace swooped me up in such a tight hug that she squeezed all the words out of me.

She checked my arms and legs, and then

pulled me into a hug again, blubbering like crazy.

Sally hung onto one of my legs. Jane Ann stood back and watched, her face pale and worried.

Finally, Grace took a good look at me. Then she boxed my ears.

I yelped. I was done being happy to see Grace again.

"You said you'd be right back, William Edmonds. We thought you were wounded, or dead, or both!" she said.

"What?"

"We got word that Mother was well, but no one could tell us anything about you. The soldier who told us to wait at the Weikerts' said there was a wounded boy in the house."

"That's Abel," I told her. "He lost his hand, but I think he'll be fine," I said.

Grace took a deep, shaky breath.

Jane Ann clung to Sally and whispered in her ear.

"Are you a ghost?" Sally asked.

I knelt down and looked into Jane Ann's eyes. "I'm no ghost. If I was a ghost, it wouldn't hurt when Grace boxed my ears. And boy did it!"

The twins nodded solemnly.

I straightened up again and took a sniff from

the bottle of peppermint oil I had taken to carrying. Truth to tell, there was a powerful smell coming off of Grace. She hadn't changed her clothes or had a decent sleep in a week. She was covered in mud and muck.

"I'm sorry I scared you," I told her. "I had to find help for Abel, and then there was no way to get back. I brought him here when the Rebs cleared out."

"Hmmpf."

"Mother's at the Christian Commission, getting supplies. I'll set up a tub in the backyard for the twins," I said. "You'll be all fresh and clean when she gets back."

For the first time in a week, Grace thought about her appearance. Her eyes flew from the cellar doors to her red shawl hanging over the front door and back again.

"No one touched your clothes," I told her. "They're hanging over the woodpile right in the cellar where you left them."

Grace put her hands on her hips. "If you expect me to bathe in the yard—"

"I'll bring some hot water to the cellar for you,"

"Yes, you will," she said. She was as bossy as ever, but a smile played on the corner of her lips.

I smiled, too. "Just make yourself presentable before you scare somebody to death."

I was out of reach before she could box my ears again.

My reunion with my sisters wasn't the last I was to have that week. On Saturday, Colonel Braxton came to call.

I had gone out to the Bailey farm to collect Molasses. She weathered the battle in a secret room under the Baileys' barn, along with their own horses. She spent an entire week in the dark, but she was safe. If the ordeal had made Molasses frightful or skittish, I couldn't see it. She was as steady as ever.

I rode into town and spotted the flag flying in the middle of the Diamond. Someone had built a new flagpole. I was proud to see it there.

Most of the houses had taken down their red flags, but every church, hotel, and public building was still a hospital. We kept Abel with us, but the rest of our men moved to the Presbyterian Church.

The town's telegraph equipment was back, and one of the first telegrams to arrive was from Father, asking about our welfare. He had good news to share, too—Jacob had been released! He and Father were together in Washington, and as soon as Jacob was strong enough to travel, they would be on the first train home.

They would find Gettysburg changed. As I rode up Baltimore Street I passed a photographer from New York City who was taking a picture of an artillery shell still stuck in the side of a house. Two Sisters of Mercy carried supplies into the Catholic Church. Mrs. Shriver was showing a gawker the bullet holes in her house and the garret window Rebel sharpshooters had used to fire on the Union men on Cemetery Hill.

"Two of them died right behind that window," I heard her say.

Every home in town carried battle scars. My own escaped with just a couple of bullet holes, but our carriage house and fence had both been torn up for barricades.

It was a pleasure to put Molasses back into her own stall, even if the wall wasn't fully there. Abel got out of bed for the first time. He sat in a chair in the sunshine and watched me brush her until her coat shone, and I could tell she had missed the attention.

Mother said Abel's recovery was a pure miracle.

There was no more fever. His wound was not yet healed, but it showed no signs of gangrene.

I pointed to his bandage

"Does it hurt much?" I asked.

"Funny thing," Abel said, "it's like my fingers hurt, even though they're gone. But the wound only itches."

"Jacob's whole arm is gone," I told him.

He nodded. "I'm right lucky I'll still be able to push a plow," he said. "But the little ones will have to do most of the harvesting."

I patted Molasses on the nose and she whinnied. "She's happy to be home," I said.

Abel nodded. "It's about time I think on getting home my own self," he said.

"What? You're not healed yet." Abel had only been with us for a week or so, but he was already a member of the family. The twins liked him better than they did me, and Grace didn't dare correct his speech or tug on his hair or order him about.

"Healed enough to sit on a train. It's time for me to get home to my own mama. She's been fending for herself for too long now."

I continued to pet Molasses, thinking of ways I could change his mind.

"You can't take a train all the way home," I said. "How are you gonna get into the South?"

Abel shrugged. "I reckon I can get a train to Washington. From there I'll cross into Virginia. Walk."

"You're not going to be a soldier again, are you?"

From everything we read in the papers, the defeat at Gettysburg had been a crushing blow to the Southern army. The day after they lost the battle here, Vicksburg, Mississippi, fell to the Union, too. But somehow, the South fought on.

I remembered that long line of Rebels I had seen on the last day of the battle. The ones that kept coming and coming and coming even though they knew they were about to be slaughtered. Would the South fight until every last one of them was dead? Would Abel?

He was quiet for some time.

"Are you?" I asked again.

Finally, he shook his head and sighed. "Ain't much use for a one-handed drummer. Can't shoot neither. I don't think the North has any right to tell the South what's what, but I'm not going to fight that war any longer."

I hadn't changed my views either. "The states

have to stick together," I said. "They can't just up and leave the Union every time they don't like something. My great grandfather fought to free our country from England. *All* the colonies fought together for what was right. What will happen to our country if the South wins and cuts us in half?"

"You think the country as a whole is more important than the states. That's not so," Abel said. "Who's in charge in your house?"

I snorted. "Grace."

Abel frowned. "No. Your papa, right?"

"Right," I said.

"What if the town came into your house and said your papa wasn't in charge anymore? Started telling you what to do."

I wouldn't like that—not at all. I had to think for a minute. "If my papa was doing something wrong, maybe that would be the right thing. And slavery's wrong. You said so yourself."

"I said my people didn't own any slaves. I don't know if it's wrong or right. I'd rather be a slave in the South than be stuck in one of your Northern factories, or one of your mines. You think those folks have it any better than our slaves?"

I didn't know anything about factories or

mines, but I knew that in the North people got paid for their work. "They get wages," I said. "And they can leave any time."

Abel simply looked at me.

I knew we could argue over this forever and never reach an agreement. But we didn't have to fight over it either. I could disagree with Abel without wanting to kill him. Why couldn't the North and the South?

"You know, my mother's going to try and keep you here until the war's over and you can take a train all the way home," I said.

"I know," Abel said with a grin. "But as soon as I'm strong enough, she'll let me go just the same."

We were walking into the kitchen when we heard a knock on the front door. Mother showed Colonel Braxton—now Brigadier General Braxton—into the parlor. He had been wounded in the leg on that third day, in what folks had begun to call Pickett's Charge, and he walked with a slight limp.

He seemed way too big for the parlor chair. It was as if he didn't belong in regular houses, like he was more fit for the battlefield than supper tables.

Grace brought in a pot of tea and sat down, too, simpering like he was her beau or something.

After thanking Abel and me for our service to him, he turned to Mother. "I was very impressed with your son's bravery and his presence of mind."

I sat up a little straighter. Was I going to get a medal? Would I stand on a podium in the Diamond while people made pretty speeches about me? The general would slip a medal around my neck, a band would launch into "The Star-Spangled Banner," and everyone would applaud.

That was an old daydream. Suddenly I wondered whether I still wanted that kind of recognition. I still believed that the Union had to stay together, and the South forced us to fight when they fired on the flag. But I wished there was another way—other than killing—to end the war.

I was still pondering those matters when General Braxton asked me to help him see if his saber was still buried in the garden.

We knelt in the dirt, running our hands through the trampled earth until my fingers found his uniform, wrapped around his rifle and his saber.

His saber wasn't the only thing he wanted.

"I'm leaving Gettysburg tomorrow and I'd like to take you with me. I need an aide. Someone to handle my papers. Act as my messenger. A boy who can keep his head in tough situations."

I hesitated. I knew the general's offer was a great honor. But it was not one I wanted—not anymore.

"You won't be on the battle lines. There will be no immediate danger."

I remembered trying to get Grace and the little ones away from the fighting. But there had been fighting—immediate danger—everywhere we turned. Battle lines had a habit of moving.

"You would be doing a fine service for your country," General Braxton said.

"I'm proud to be asked," I said slowly. I thought about all those daydreams I had about bringing glory to my family and to my country. Part of me wanted that. Sometimes my fingers still itched to rattle a drum, to load a musket, to wave the flag.

Then I considered the destruction around Gettysburg, and the death. Death wasn't glorious. It was scary and ugly, and it seemed as if it hadn't changed a thing. The war kept on. Those of us left behind had to bury the bodies, send on the unfinished letters, and greet the family members who came looking for their dead.

I almost told him that my parents would never

agree to such a scheme, and that was true. But there was another truth, too. "I'm all for the Union, but I don't believe that men standing on opposite sides and shooting each other to death can rightly decide any question."

He looked for a moment as if he might disagree, but then he nodded. "I trust you'll be in touch if you change your mind."

"Where do you go from here?" I asked.

"We're following Lee's men south," he said. Then he wiped the dirt off his saber and handed it to me. "With my thanks."

We were silent as I walked him to the street.

The general shook my hand and said good-bye.

"Be safe," I said.

★ CHAPTER TWENTY-THREE ★

A New Birth of Freedom

November 18-19, 1863

A few weeks after the battle ended people began to speak of a new cemetery for the fallen soldiers. Most had been buried where they fell. Soon land was bought and bodies were brought from all parts of the battlefield to be reburied there.

The greatest orator in the country, Edward Everett, was to make a speech. Even more exciting, President Lincoln agreed to come and say a few words at the dedication ceremony.

The first frost had put an end to the terrible stench, but you could still see signs of the battle everywhere.

In the days leading up to the exercises, Gettysburg was once again crowded with people. The hotels were overflowing, and every house had guests. Father's cousins from New Jersey were with us, along with the family of one of the Union men Mother had taken care of during the battle. You could scarce take a step in the night without stepping on someone, and the men had to sleep sitting up in the parlor.

I wished Abel were still here, but we had finally gotten a letter that told us he made it safely home to his mama. He asked me to visit him when the war ended, and I wrote back that I would.

Mother and Grace made a feast the night before the exercises. Farmers said it would take three years before they had fully replaced all that was lost to the Rebels' raids and to the battle, but we had food enough. Turkey and plum pudding were on the menu, along with sweet potatoes, onions, apples, and sweet pickles. I snatched a pickle every chance I got. Of course Grace spied me.

"Leave some for the rest of the party," she snapped.

I stuck my tongue out at her.

She sighed and turned to Mother. "He's such a child."

I rolled my eyes at Jacob, and he grinned. Grace had been a little in awe of him when he first came home, but it wasn't long before she started bossing him around, too. He had started in at the college and intended to become a minister.

"Are you sorry you can't be a doctor like Father?" I asked. That's what he wanted to be before the war.

Jacob shook his head. "I've seen enough blood. Besides, people won't object to a one-armed preacher."

"Don't get all dried up and serious like some preachers," I told him.

"Or some sisters," he joked.

Grace stuck her tongue out at him, and he laughed.

Jacob and I had had many talks about the war. I was afraid he wouldn't look kindly on the fact that I had made friends with a Rebel and taken him in, but Jacob said he made Rebel friends of his own.

"This war was unavoidable," he told me. "The debate about states rights versus a strong federal government has been going on since George Washington's day. Slavery is the cause that brought it to a head, but it's been coming for a long time."

"Will it end soon, do you think?" I asked.

Jacob took a deep breath and let it out again. "The South isn't giving up, are they?" he asked.

I shook my head.

He put his hand on my shoulder. "They'll run out of men long before we do," he said. "The North is better equipped to fight, but the South has a stronger commitment to their cause."

I sat at my bedroom window that night thinking about those things and about the next day's exercises. People paraded up and down the street all night, unable to find a place to sleep. I hadn't gotten to the train station in time to see the president's arrival, but I fully intended to see him at the ceremony the next day.

I wondered if he would see me in the crowd. I imagined the people parting as he walked toward me. "You must be the boy I have heard about," he'd say. "The one who escaped across enemy lines and helped win the battle."

"I was proud to do it, sir," I'd answer. "I only wish that winning the battle would have brought the war to an end."

"We all long for peace," the president would say. "But some causes are worth fighting for."

The next thing I knew the sun was up and I had a crick in my neck from sleeping on the windowsill.

As soon as I could, I escaped all the hubbub at home and raced down to the Diamond. President Lincoln was staying at the home of David Wills, and I hoped to get a glimpse of him. My strongest wish was to shake his hand.

Around ten o'clock, Mr. Lincoln came out of the house and mounted his horse. A column rode up Baltimore Street with the president at the center. I ran beside them, keeping him in my sight. His horse was medium-sized and the president was very tall. His legs dangled, almost touching the ground, but he appeared to be a fine horseman.

I lost my place at his side when the procession turned into the new cemetery. Even so, I managed to squeeze my way through the crowd to the platform where the exercises were to be held. I stood right at the bottom of the stairs and hooked my arm around the railing so that no one could push me away.

Edward Everett spoke first. He talked all about the battle and the town and the brave work the townspeople had done in caring for the wounded.

It was a fine speech and a long one, but I barely listened. I was watching the president.

Mr. Lincoln's face was lined and sad, but his expression was kindly. Finally, Mr. Everett finished. While the band played, Mr. Lincoln reached into his side pocket and drew out a case containing a pair of spectacles. Then reaching into his pocket again, he drew out a sheet of crumpled paper.

He looked taller than ever when he stood. He walked to the front of the platform and began to speak. I held my breath, listening.

Four score and seven years ago our fathers brought forth on this continent a new nation, conceived in liberty, and dedicated to the proposition that all men are created equal.

Now we are engaged in a great civil war, testing whether that nation, or any nation so conceived and so dedicated, can long endure. We are met on a great battle-field of that war. We have come to dedicate a portion of that field, as a final resting-place for those who here gave their lives that that nation might live. It is altogether fitting and proper that we should do this.

But, in a larger sense, we can not dedicate . . . we can not consecrate . . . we can not hallow . . . this ground. The brave men, living and dead, who strug-

gled here, have consecrated it far above our poor power to add or detract. The world will little note, nor long remember what we say here, but it can never forget what they did here. It is for us, the living, rather, to be dedicated here to the unfinished work which they who fought here have thus far so nobly advanced. It is rather for us to be here dedicated to the great task remaining before us . . . that from these honored dead we take increased devotion to that cause for which they gave the last full measure of devotion; that we here highly resolve that these dead shall not have died in vain; that this nation, under God, shall have a new birth of freedom; and that government of the people, by the people, for the people, shall not perish from the earth.

It was over almost before I knew it. Indeed, the audience did not clap for a full minute, expecting the president to continue speaking, but he had already turned to the others on the platform and began shaking hands.

I barely had time to absorb his words before the party began to leave the stage. Descending the stairs, the president's eyes came into contact with mine. He held out his hand as he passed by and said, "Hello, young man, who are you?"

I grasped his hand. My face flushed and my

throat closed up, but I managed to squeak, "I am Will Edmonds."

And then he was gone, swallowed up by the crowd.

I watched them go, stunned that I had actually gotten to shake the president's hand. I was still turning his words over in my mind.

" . . . government of the people, by the people, for the people, shall not perish from the earth," I whispered to myself.

I was glad I had not gone to war with Colonel Braxton. I was glad I did not have to face another battle. I was still a boy, and shooting and dying was the work of men. Still, I believed what the president said—that our Union shall not perish. If my country needed me to fight for her another day, I would do it. But I hoped it would not be necessary. I hoped I could spend my life waging peace, not war.

Today my job was only this—to go home and let Grace know that I had shaken the president's hand, and she had not. That and to give thanks that my family was safe. All of us. Together.

★ HISTORICAL NOTE ★

The Battle of Gettysburg was the biggest, bloodiest battle ever fought on North American soil. More than 150,000 men waged war on the rocky hills, wheat fields, orchards, and ridges surrounding the town and in the town itself.

Gettysburg resulted in the highest number of casualties in any battle of the Civil War. More than 50,000 men were killed or wounded. Not all of the casualties were soldiers. Trees were shot so full of bullets that they died of lead poisoning.

The town of Gettysburg and its 2,400 citizens found themselves in the middle of two vast armies. The experiences of those people were the inspiration for this story. William Edmonds and his family are fictional characters set down in the middle of real events. You might be wondering how much of Will's story is true and how much is fiction.

Many of Gettysburg's citizens wrote about their experiences in the battle, and I relied on their firsthand accounts to tell Will's story. I used many sources, but Will's experiences are based largely on those of two of Gettysburg's young citizens.

Daniel Skelly, a seventeen-year-old clerk, watched the battle begin from a high branch on an oak tree on Seminary Hill. Later that morning he escorted General Howard to the observatory on the top of the Fahnestock Brothers store, as Will does in this novel.

Tillie Pierce was fifteen when the fighting broke out. Her neighbor, Henrietta "Hettie" Shriver, asked Tillie to go with her and her two young daughters to Mrs. Shriver's parents' farm on the Taneytown Road when the battle began. Mrs.

Shriver thought they would be safer there. Instead, they found themselves on the front lines.

The Rebels did indeed thunder into town shooting and hollering on June 26, 1863.

Some of them captured a group of African-Americans with plans to sell them in the South. There is no record of anyone trying to stop the Rebels, as Will does in this story, but at least one black woman did manage to escape and hide in a church belfry. The fate of the rest of the captured people is still unknown today.

More than a few Union soldiers found hiding places in Gettysburg during the retreat of July 1. Most famously, General Alexander Schimmelfennig hid in the Garlach family's woodshed from July 1 until the morning of July 4. The Garlachs kept his presence a secret and slipped him food when they could. This was dangerous. They were surrounded by Confederate troops and could have been shot for helping a Union soldier.

I didn't come across any records of Union soldiers slipping across enemy lines to rejoin their comrades, but I like to think that one or two might have tried—perhaps with the aid of one of Gettysburg's brave citizens. That inspired me to invent the story of Will's dangerous journey across the Rebel lines with the fictional Colonel Braxton.

The Battle of Gettysburg proved to be a major turning point in the war. The South lost one-third of its army and never regained its full fighting strength. In addition, the battle had exactly the opposite effect on the North than Robert E. Lee had hoped.

Before the battle, some Northerners had begun to pressure President Abraham Lincoln to negotiate a peace with the South. But the Union victory, coupled with their anger over Lee's invasion of a Northern state, caused many of them to renew their support of the president and the war.

The war lasted for two more years, but the Confederate defeat at Gettysburg, followed by the fall of Vicksburg, Mississippi, the next day, was the beginning of the end for the Confederacy.

CHILDREN'S ROLES *in the*
★ CIVIL WAR ★

More than three million Americans fought in the Civil War, and over 600,000 men died in it. Battles were fought in over 10,000 places, primarily in the South. Armies swept across farms and burned towns. Homes became military headquarters. Churches and schoolhouses were turned into hospitals.

Never before had civilians been exposed to war and suffering the way they were in this war, when the fighting was in their own backyards. As a result, children played an important role in the Civil War.

Girls and their mothers took their brothers' and fathers' places in fields and factories when the men went off to war. Some girls even disguised themselves as boys to serve in the armies on both sides.

Many girls had no choice but to become nurses when wounded soldiers needed help. Gettysburg resident Sadie Bushman was just nine years old when an army surgeon asked her to hold a cup of water to a soldier's mouth while he sawed off the man's leg. Sadie assisted that doctor for weeks, until every last wounded soldier left Gettysburg.

When the war began, the minimum age to join the Union army was eighteen. But many soldiers, especially in the South and at the end of the war, were barely into their teens. Some boys thought war would be a great adventure and lied about their ages, or used false names in order to become soldiers. Others joined with their fathers and became drummers and musicians. These musicians were vitally important. Drums were used to send signals to troops in battle and at camp.

Some of those boys paid for their military service with their lives. Six boys earned our nation's highest military award—the Medal of Honor. One of them, William "Willie" Johnston, was eleven when he saw his first action during the Peninsular Campaign of 1862. He was a drummer for the 3rd Vermont Infantry. Willie managed to hold on to his drum in a desperate retreat and was personally thanked by President Lincoln.

The children who happened to live on the battles' front lines were forced to grow up fast and take on adult roles. They were ordinary children living in extraordinary times, and they rose to the occasion with grace and courage.

★ HISTORIC CHARACTERS ★

Some of the characters in Will at the Battle of Gettysburg, 1863, *were real people who played a part in the Civil War.*

Brigadier General John Buford was the commander of a cavalry division in the Union army. Buford's troops rode into Gettysburg on Tuesday, June 30, 1863. He stayed in the area overnight and waited for the Confederates to return. His decision to stay in Gettysburg set the stage for the battle to begin the following day.

Jefferson Davis, a graduate of West Point, was a plantation owner in Mississippi. He also served in Congress. Davis became the president of the Confederate States of America when the Southern states seceded from the Union.

Edward Everett was the leading speaker of his day. He had a long political career as a congressman and senator as well as governor of Massachusetts.

Major General Joseph Hooker, known as "Fighting Joe," was a commander of the Union army. He was defeated by Confederate General Robert E. Lee at the Battle of Chancellorsville in May 1863. President Lincoln replaced him with General Meade a few days before the Battle of Gettysburg.

General Oliver O. Howard served in the Union army. He surveyed the Gettysburg battlefield from the observation deck of the Fahnestock Brothers store on the morning of July 1, 1863. He took charge of the battlefield after the death of General Reynolds.

General Robert E. Lee, the son of Revolutionary War hero "Light-Horse Harry" Lee, was a top graduate of the West Point Military Academy. He served in the United States army for thirty-two years, but resigned when his home state of Virginia seceded from the Union. As commander of the Confederate army he won a series of battles against the Union. His army seemed unbeatable when they marched into the North in 1863. The Union victory against Lee's forces at the Battle of Gettysburg was a major turning point in the war. Lee's army retreated south and never again fought in the Northern states.

Abraham Lincoln, the president of the United States, visited Gettysburg and gave his famous address in November, 1863.

Albertus McCreary, fifteen, lived in Gettysburg. During the battle he wore a blue soldier's cap and was nearly taken prisoner by the Confederates. A number of his neighbors came to his rescue and assured the Rebels he was not a soldier. After the battle, McCreary sold tobacco to Union soldiers and battlefield souvenirs to tourists.

Charlie McCurdy was ten years old and lived across the street from Petey Winter's sweet shop at the time of the battle. He watched a Rebel soldier fill his hat with candy through the store's window. When the soldier came outside, he gave a grateful Charlie a handful of candy.

Mary McLean was six years old during the Battle of Gettysburg. She did indeed stick her head out of a window and sing, "Hang Jeff Davis from a sour apple tree," to the Confederate soldiers on the street below. Her father worried the house would be destroyed, but the Rebel soldiers only laughed.

Major General George Gordon Meade, commander of the Union army at the Battle of Gettysburg, was asked to take command just three days before the battle. His men called him the "Snapping Turtle."

Matilda "Tillie" Pierce was born in Gettysburg in 1848. She was fifteen when the fighting began. In hopes of escaping danger, she traveled to the Weikert farm outside of town with her neighbor Mrs. Shriver. She had no idea that she would find herself in the middle of some of the worst fighting of the three-day battle.

General John Reynolds was offered the command of the Union army several days before the Battle of Gettysburg. He turned it down, and General Meade was appointed instead. Reynolds was killed on July 1st leading his troops into battle.

Henrietta "Hettie" Shriver left her home on Baltimore Street with her two young children and her neighbor Tillie Pierce when the battle began. She traveled to her parents' farm on the Taneytown Road near the hills known as the Round Tops, the scene of some of the fiercest fighting.

Daniel Skelly was a seventeen-year-old clerk at the Fahnestock Brothers store. He watched the battle begin from a tall oak tree on Seminary Hill and escorted General Howard to the store's observation deck on the morning of July 1.

Brigadier General J.E.B. Stuart, a Confederate officer and the most famous horseman of the Civil War, led Lee's cavalry. He did not arrive at Gettysburg until long after the battle started. Stuart's horsemen were defeated in fighting three miles east of Gettysburg on the afternoon of July 3rd. He retreated south with the rest of Lee's army but was killed later in the war.

Virginia "Jennie" Wade was the only civilian killed during the battle. On the morning of July 3, while kneading bread dough for hungry soldiers, she was hit by a stray bullet and died.

Jacob and Sarah Weikert, Hettie Shriver's parents, saw their farm overrun by soldiers during the battle. Like many of the homes and farms in and around Gettysburg, theirs became a hospital for thousands of wounded.

★ TIMELINE ★
The Battle of Gettysburg and the American Civil War

1860

April 5   Abraham Lincoln is elected president of
                 the United States. Southerners believe
                 he will stamp out slavery in the South.

December 20   South Carolina votes to secede from the
                 United States.

1861

January-February Mississippi, Florida, Alabama, Georgia,
                 Louisiana, and Texas join South Carolina
                 to form the Confederate States of
                 America.

February 18   Jefferson Davis is inaugurated as presi-
                 dent of the Confederacy. He later said:
                 "Our cause was so just, so sacred, that
                 had I known all that has come to pass,
                 had I known what was to be inflicted
                 upon me, all that my country was to
                 suffer, all that our posterity was to
                 endure, I would do it all over again."

March 4   Abraham Lincoln is inaugurated as presi-
                 dent of the United States. He declares

that no state has the right to leave the United States and that "the Union is unbroken."

April 12	Confederates open fire on Union forces at Fort Sumter in Charleston Harbor, South Carolina. No one on either side was killed, but Union troops were forced to surrender.
April 15	Lincoln calls for 75,000 volunteers to fight the Confederates.
April 17-May 20	Virginia, Arkansas, Tennessee, and North Carolina join the Confederacy.
April 20	Robert E. Lee leaves the United States army to fight for the South. In early 1861, President Abraham Lincoln had invited Lee to take command of the entire Union army. Lee believed it was his duty to fight for his home state of Virginia, even though he thought secession was wrong.
July 21	Union and Confederate forces meet for the first time in a full battle near Bull Run Creek in Manassas, Virginia. The Battle of Bull Run, known as Manassas in the South, is a Rebel victory.

1862

February   Ulysses S. Grant captures Forts Henry and Donelson in Tennessee for the Union. After the victory, he became known as "Unconditional Surrender" Grant, because he refused to negotiate with the Rebels. He was President Lincoln's most successful general.

March 17   The Union army sets sail to Virginia's York-James Peninsula, beginning the Peninsular Campaign. They planned to fight their way west to Richmond, the Confederate capital.

April 6-7   The Union wins the Battle of Shiloh, Tennessee, but with enormous losses.

April 25   The Union captures New Orleans, Louisiana.

May-June   Confederate General Stonewall Jackson's Shenandoah Valley Campaign results in a Southern victory.

June 25   The Seven Days' Battles begin. They end on July 1, bringing an end to the Peninsular Campaign. Union troops escaped destruction, but the Confederates were the real victors.

August 29-30	The Confederates defeat Union troops again at the Second Battle of Bull Run.
September	General Robert E. Lee marches his army into Maryland, a Union state. Lee's forces meet the Union's Army of the Potomac near the town of Sharpsburg and Antietam Creek on September 17. The Battle of Antietam, a Northern victory, is the bloodiest day of fighting in the entire Civil War. Twenty-three thousand troops are killed or wounded.
September 22	Lincoln announces the Emancipation Proclamation, warning the Rebel states that unless they return to the Union by January 1, 1863, their slaves will be "forever free." Slaves in Union states, like Maryland, were not freed.
December 13	The Confederates win the Battle of Fredericksburg, Virginia. The Union suffers 12,700 casualties.

1863

January 1	President Lincoln signs the Emancipation Proclamation, ending slavery in the Confederate states. Congress later took steps to make sure that slavery was abolished permanently in all the states.

The Thirteenth Amendment to the Constitution declared that "Neither slavery nor involuntary servitude . . . shal exist within the United States."

April 16

Ulysses S. Grant launches his campaign to capture Vicksburg, Mississippi.

May 1-4

Robert E. Lee's army of 60,000 men defeat 130,000 Union troops at Chancellorsville, Virginia. It is Lee's greatest victory, but also a costly one. He loses nearly one quarter of his army.

June

Robert E. Lee launches his second invasion of the North, marching his soldiers through Maryland and into Pennsylvania.

June 26

Rebel cavalry ride into Gettysburg, followed by 5,000 infantry soldiers. They demand money and supplies.

June 27

Four Union scouts ride into Gettysburg, practically on the heels of the departing Rebels.

June 28

Union cavalry arrive in Gettysburg. Over the next few days, both Confederate and Union troops march toward the town.

July 1-3	The Battle of Gettysburg begins when Union cavalry makes contact with Confederate troops on McPherson's Ridge to the west of the town. The fighting lasts for three days, resulting in the bloodiest battle of the entire war and a Union victory.
July 4	Lee begins his retreat to Virginia. On the same day, Vicksburg, Mississippi, surrenders to the Union. The Mississippi River is now in the hands of the Union.
September 19-20	Confederates win the Battle of Chickamauga, Georgia.
November 19	A national cemetery is dedicated at Gettysburg, Pennsylvania. President Lincoln gives his famous address. He talks about the ideals behind the founding of the United States—freedom and equality. He also declares his commitment that the "government of the people, by the people, for the people, shall not perish from the earth."
November 23-25	Union troops win the Battle of Chattanooga, Tennessee.

1864

May 5-6	The Battle of the Wilderness in Virginia is the first of a bloody series of skirmishes between Ulysses S. Grant and Robert E. Lee.
May 7	Union General William Sherman begins his campaign to capture Atlanta, the South's railroad and supply center. This will cripple the Confederate army.
July 22	Sherman wins the Battle of Atlanta for the Union.
November 8	Abraham Lincoln is reelected president.
November 15	Sherman burns Atlanta and begins his famous March to the Sea.
December 21	Savannah, Georgia, surrenders to Sherman's army.

1865

January 31	Congress passes the Thirteenth Amendment, abolishing slavery in the United States. After the war, the former Confederate states ratified the amendment in order to regain representation in Congress.

| March 4 | In President Lincoln's second inaugural address, with the end of the war in sight, he calls for forgiveness and healing between the North and the South. "With malice toward none; with charity for all; with firmness in the right, as God gives us to see the right, let us strive on to finish the work we are in; to bind up the nation's wounds; to care for him who shall have borne the battle, and for his widow, and his orphan—to do all which may achieve and cherish a just, and a lasting peace, among ourselves, and with all nations." |

| April 2 | Union troops occupy Richmond, Virginia, the capital of the South. |

| April 9 | Robert E. Lee surrenders to Ulysses S. Grant at Appomattox Court House, Virginia. |

| April 14 | John Wilkes Booth shoots President Lincoln at Ford's Theatre. Lincoln dies the next day and is succeeded by his vice president, Andrew Johnson. |

| May 10 | Jefferson Davis is captured by federal troops. President Johnson declares the rebellion over. Many people in the South |

were deeply disappointed that they had lost the War for Southern Independence. They saw it as a blow to the liberty their ancestors had fought for in the American Revolution. A long and difficult reconstruction period began when the war ended.

★ GLOSSARY ★

abolitionist: A person who wanted to end slavery.

artillery: Large guns, including cannons.

belfry: A bell tower on the top of a building.

Bluebellies: A slang term for Union soldiers, who wore blue uniforms.

caisson: A wagon used to hold ammunition.

cavalry: Soldiers who fought on horseback.

confectionery: A sweet shop, like a candy store or a bakery.

Confederate: A supporter of the Southern states, known as the Confederate States of America.

Copperheads: During the Civil War, people in the North who wanted to make peace with the Confederates instead of waging war to force them to remain in the Union.

crossroads: The intersection of two or more roads.

double-quick: A fast march, at double time.

field glasses: Binoculars.

garret: Attic.

greenback: A dollar bill—paper money.

inaugurate: To induct, or swear someone into office. When presidents are inaugurated, they often give a speech known as an inaugural address.

infantry: Soldiers who fought and marched on foot.

Mason-Dixon Line: The invisible line that established the boundaries between Pennsylvania, Maryland, Delaware, and Virginia. It divided the North and the South, the free and the slave states. The line was named after the two men who surveyed the land in a border dispute.

muster in: Join the military. Soldiers were said to "muster in" when they enrolled in the army.

parole: Release a prisoner. The Rebels paroled their civilian prisoners when they left Gettysburg on June 27, 1863.

picket: A soldier in front of the main fighting force who acted as a guard. Picket soldiers were the first to see enemy movements. They were also the targets of sharpshooters.

portico: A porch with columns.

privy: A bathroom in a small shed outside—an outhouse.

proclamation: An official announcement.

Rebel: A term people in the North used to describe the Southern soldiers.

scout: A soldier sent out ahead of the main fighting force to gather information about the enemy.

secede: Withdraw, or leave. The Southern states voted to secede from the Union.

sharpshooter: A shooter who had very good aim over long distances. Sharpshooters took positions on hilltops and attics to shoot at the enemy.

skirmish: A small battle or military action.

valise: A suitcase.

★ FURTHER READING ★
Want to learn more about the Civil War?
Here are some great nonfiction sources.

At Gettysburg, or What a Girl Saw and Heard of the Battle by Tillie Pierce Alleman, published in 1888. Reprinted and distributed by Butternut and Blue and Stan Clark Military Books. Tillie Pierce's eyewitness account of the battle.

Fields of Fury: The American Civil War by James McPherson, published by Atheneum Books for Young Readers, 2002. An excellent overview of the entire war.

Eyewitness: Civil War by John Stanchack, published by Dorling Kindersley Books, 2000. A photo-filled guide to the sites, people, and artifacts of the Civil War.

Harriet Tubman, Secret Agent: How Daring Slaves and Free Blacks Spied for the Union During the Civil War by Thomas B. Allen, published by National Geographic, 2006.

The Long Road to Gettysburg by Jim Murphy, published by Clarion Books, 1992. Firsthand accounts by Confederate Lieutenant John Dooley, age eighteen, and Union soldier Thomas Galway, just fifteen.

When Johnny Went Marching: Young Americans Fight the Civil War by G. Clifton Wisler, published by HarperCollins Publishers, 2001. The stories of forty-nine young people—soldiers and spies, drummers and buglers, boys and girls—who got caught up in the War Between the States.

Acknowledgments

Special thanks to Martha Levine and Chris Dubois for driving me around the battlefield and putting up with me while I prowled the streets of Gettysburg looking for Will's story.

I am immensely grateful to the people of Gettysburg. They not only lived through the bloodiest battle of the Civil War, but then took the time to put their experiences down on paper. This book would not have been possible without their stories. Nor would it have been possible without the generous people of present-day Gettysburg—the Adams County Historical Society, walking tour guides, museum docents, park rangers, and others—who helped me step back in time and shared their favorite stories with me.

Deepest thanks go to my first readers, Josanne LaValley, Kekla Magoon, Bethany Hegedus, and Constance Foland, and especially to Margaret Woollatt, who edited the manuscript with such a careful eye.